THE DOUBLE-EDGED SWORD

Titles by Ian Whates

THE DARK ANGELS (NewCon Press):
Pelquin's Comet (2015)
The Ion Raider (2017)
Dark Angels Rising (2020)

THE CITY OF 100 ROWS (Angry Robot):
City of Dreams and Nightmare (2011)
City of Hope and Despair (2012)
City of Light and Shadow (2013)

THE NOISE (Solaris):
The Noise Within (2010)
The Noise Revealed (2011)

COLLECTIONS:
The Gift of Joy (2009) *(NewCon Press)*
Growing Pains (2013) *(PS Publishing)*
Dark Travellings (2016) *(Fox Spirit)*
Wourism & Other Stories (2019) *(Luna Press)*

NOVELLAS:
The Smallest of Things (2018) *(PS Publishing)*

Co-written with Tim C. Taylor
THE HUMAN LEGION:
Human Empire (2015)
The War Against the White Knights (2016)

THE DOUBLE-EDGED SWORD

A TALE OF THE FALLEN HERO

Ian Whates

NEWCON
PRESS

NewCon Press
England

First published in December 2022 by NewCon Press,
41 Wheatsheaf Road, Alconbury Weston, Cambs, PE28 4LF

NCP295 (limited edition hardback)
NCP296 (softback)

10 9 8 7 6 5 4 3 2 1

"Not a Moment to Swoon" originally appeared in *Afterburn SF*, 2006. All other material is previously unpublished.

ISBN:

978-1-914953-40-8 (hardback)
978-1-914953-41-5 (softback)

Cover Image by Lidia B from Pixabay

Typesetting by Ian Whates

One:
Not a Moment to Swoon

The voice came from behind me. "It *is* you, isn't it," which has always struck me as a ludicrous phrase.

"Oh, it's me all right," I assured him, which brought us no closer to establishing whether the 'me' I was referring to was the same as the 'you' he thought me to be. Unfortunately, it turned out that I was.

I'd spotted him across the taproom earlier, looking at me with an air of puzzled concentration that has become all-too-familiar in recent years.

A pity; the Golden Bear had seemed such a perfect place in which to hole up for a while and certainly the ale was more than acceptable. I had come to Cullen Ford – a small town at the toe end of nowhere – to lie low and recuperate after a particularly unsavoury incident which I prefer not to dwell on. It seemed ideally suited to purpose, or had done up until now.

I decided to call it a night and head back to the hovel – described imaginatively as 'lodgings' – where I was staying, before my curious observer connected the dots and stoked up enough liquid courage to come over and satisfy his curiosity. Too late. With the door just a few tantalising steps away, he approached me with that meaningless truism.

So here I was, about to be drawn into a conversation I had no desire to be a part of, wondering whether it would end in violence this time, or just rudeness.

"You don't remember me, do you?" At least that was one thing we could agree on. "No reason why you should, of course,

I was just a boy back then." He seemed little more than that now – fresh faced, sandy hair, the suggestion of freckles and the sort of wide-eyed innocence that never lasts long in the big bad world. "My mother took me to see you. It was at Trilmouth."

I groaned. Of course it was; how could it possibly have been anywhere else?

He was still yapping, "To be honest, she didn't take me to see you, as such. She really went to see..."

"Gerard," I cut in.

"Yes, how did you know?"

"Because that's *always* why the women came to see us: to catch a glimpse of our esteemed leader."

"Look, please let me buy you a drink. There were so many outrageous rumours and claims at the time… I've always wanted to hear what *really* happened."

That was my cue. I should have left then – made my excuses and run, but a free drink is pretty hard to resist. For a moment I stood there, poised on the cusp of indecision, torn between the conflicting urges of thirst and common sense. Thirst won. It usually does.

At least I could enjoy some more of that very palatable ale, even if it did mean reliving the events that led to my being thrown in jail.

Fleas. That was my enduring memory of jail: filth, the stench, uncomfortably hirsute blankets and, above all else, fleas. Thankfully he did *not* want to hear about that period. Rather, it was the episode that brought about my disgrace that interested him. Which was bad enough.

"Was Gerard really as magnificent as they say?"

Another suppressed groan. Oh well, he was paying. "Gerard was certainly magnificent to look at," I conceded. "Tall, bronzed, well-muscled with golden hair..."

"A great, great hero."

I snorted, "Yeah, right. He was awkward with a bow, a passably good swordsman and a hopeless strategist – some hero."

Predictably, that surprised him. The Gerard I'd just described was at odds with the one painted by popular myth in every way, which was a tremendous tribute to the man's true genius: the ability to manipulate his own public image.

"Awkward…? *Passable*? Why did the rest of you follow him, in that case?"

Why indeed? No mystery really; the reasons were obvious once you took the trouble to look at them. "He had the rep," I said, which just about summed things up.

Gerard wasn't a man who ever felt the need to play down his notoriety – quite the opposite, in fact: he revelled in it, *relished* it, and we all benefited as a result.

"Don't get me wrong," I continued, "he wasn't stupid. He surrounded himself with people who were experts at the things he wasn't. I was a miles better swordsman, for example, and so was Alvin. Cedric was the best archer I've ever seen and Tam, who joined us after Cedric was killed at Arden Falls, wasn't far behind. Jaeko was a master at planning and strategy and old Sirus had a few tricks that had to be seen to be believed. Claimed they were sorcery and they probably were, if you give credence to that sort of thing. Each and every one of us had our uses.

"Thing was, by following Gerard we got all the plum jobs and the big rewards – the sort that none of us would ever have had a sniff at on our own. He had the reputation, you see, he was 'The Hero'. Only ever one man to call on in a crisis: Gerard."

"But surely there must have been *something* special about him," the youth insisted. "After all, he must have won that reputation somehow in the first place."

"Oh yes," I assured him, "there was something special about him all right. His power over women."

"His fabled charm."

"No," I shook my head, "it was more than that. It was like a bewitchment, a spell if you will, which he could turn on and off just like that," I snapped my fingers. "I've seen it happen. One minute we'd be getting nowhere with some stuck-up lady this or countess that, with her not giving an inch on payment rates or terms, then suddenly she would stop in mid-sentence, forget what she'd been saying and go weak at the knees. After that she'd be putty in his hands. More than once everybody had to clear the room to allow Gerard and the lady in question to indulge in some 'in-depth discussions' there and then. It was quite something."

"You really believe that? You think it was some sort of magical power?"

I shrugged and muttered, "Fairy moans."

"Pardon?"

"Oh, just something Sirus told me once. He said he reckoned it was all down to fairy moans. Maybe he was right, I never did know much about sorcery. Maybe Gerard was able to summon the voices of fairies that only women could hear, bewitching them." I shrugged, "Used to listen hard whenever I knew he was doing it... never heard any fairies though, moaning or otherwise.

"Sirus would just laugh when I told him and say I was doing it wrong, that I should have been listening with my nose, but he always was a funny old coot."

"Incredible." The lad was well and truly hooked.

"Thirsty work, this story telling," I glanced meaningfully at my now empty tankard.

"Oh... I'm sorry," he stood up. "Allow me."

With pleasure.

Ale replenished, I set about telling him what had happened, describing briefly how we had risen to prominence after a series of successful jobs, each of which led to the next one, slightly more significant than the last and correspondingly more rewarding.

Then came the big one. The council of Trilmouth approached us and asked for our help. This was major league at last, what we had been working towards. Trilmouth was one of the top trading cities. If we could make ourselves useful to them, indispensable even, then we really had cracked it.

It emerged that the Crystal of Relf had been stolen. Even I had heard of that hallowed chunk of glass. Bequeathed to the city by its founder, the 'sorcerer' King Relf, it was said to contain great power. Many believed that Trilmouth owed its success and pre-eminence entirely to the mystical properties of the crystal. However real or imagined those powers might be, the council felt the city's influence would wane without it.

To make matters worse, it had been stolen by one of their own number following a disagreement. Said to be a sorceress herself, the Lady Margeaut had snatched the crystal and fled to her castle hideaway in the mountains above the city. The council were now uncertain of whom among their own troops and contacts were to be trusted, so they turned to us.

They offered a reward larger than everything we had earned to date combined – enough that each of us could retire in reasonable comfort, if we chose to.

I described in slightly greater detail what happened on the fateful day itself – how we tricked our way into the castle, how we had penetrated deep within before being discovered and then had to fight our way after that. Swordplay in a confined space is a great leveller and as we made our way upward in pursuit of a fleetingly glimpsed woman who stayed tantalisingly out of reach, every step demanded payment in sweat and blood. Not much of it our blood, thankfully. We were good; very good.

She fled to the very roof of the highest tower and it was there that we finally cornered her.

"It was a frozen tableau," I explained, milking it, aware that he was hanging on my every word. "The lady Margeaut poised on the brink of the parapet, glorious in silk and velvet, illuminated by moonlight and sputtering torches, golden hair flowing in the wind, which whipped her dress about like some half-furled banner. Her hand was held out, suspending the precious orb over the void.

"Tam was there, staring down the shaft of an arrow pointed at her heart; me and Alvin flanked him, with swords drawn, wondering if we dared inch any closer, whilst Jeanty stood off to one side, debating whether any of his acrobatics would enable him to catch the crystal if she did drop it...

"And at the centre stood Gerard. Magnificent, Golden Gerard. The voice of reason, telling her that it was finished, insisting that if she would just step away from the edge no harm would befall her, that he personally guaranteed her safety if she would just hand over the crystal. It was working too. She was weakening, starting to discuss terms. Any fool could see that she was on the point of yielding, that she was about to give up... Well, any fool but one, apparently. Another moment and it would have been job done, but do you know what the stupid oaf did then? What the great Golden Buffoon just had to go and do?"

My audience shook his head, enthralled.

"He turned on his much-vaunted *charm*, that's what. It wasn't happening quickly enough for our Gerard, oh no. Mere words were too slow, so he had to do it the easy way, the dumb ox!" I paused, shaking with fury even now, after all these years.

"And?" I was prompted.

"She swooned. Literally collapsed. You could see the exact instant when Gerard's power hit her. One minute she stood there, beautiful and defiant, the next she just crumpled, lost her balance and toppled right over the edge, with all of us lunging to try and catch her. Jeanty even managed to grab hold of a corner of her dress, but it tore as she fell and he was left holding no more than a tatter of silk." I stopped speaking, seeing it all again, unable to go on for the moment. "Biggest purse of our lives and he had to go and do that!" I muttered at length.

"Is that when you hit him?"

I nodded, "Smack on his golden bloody chin."

"None of this ever came out," he said breathlessly.

"Of course not. Gerard was still the meal ticket after all, so the others all got together and decided to salvage what they could. Thus the official story emerged – about how we had fought valiantly through the castle to confront the evil sorceress on the roof of its highest tower, from whence she flung herself to her doom, taking the crystal with her rather than surrender it to its rightful custodians."

"But you refused to go along with that story?"

"Too true. I'm a man of principle, you see. I'd had more than enough of the Golden Gorilla and his posturing by then. Besides which," I felt obliged to concede, "that punch broke his jaw, so he wasn't too keen on having me around any more."

"Which is why you were thrown in jail."

"Yup, that's about the size of it. For assaulting the great *Hero*." I drained my tankard. "Well, there you have it – the real story of what went on. Thanks for the drinks." I went to rise. "All such a long time ago," I muttered. "The only thing I still have from those days is the ornamental dagger Gerard gave me that time when I saved his life. Of course, we were on better terms back then."

"Can I see it?" he said at once.

"The knife? Sorry, I haven't got it with me, it's back at my room."

"Oh." Obvious disappointment.

"…which isn't really that far – just around the corner, in fact, if you'd care to come back and see it."

"Would you mind?"

I shrugged, "I was going there anyway."

So we left together, with him still talking, still asking questions, which I answered in unhelpful monosyllables, my mind on other things.

It was dark already – the evenings were drawing in. As we stepped from the smoky warmth of the inn, the night greeted us with a cold slap to the cheeks. I led him through a narrow side street, badly lit, little more than an alley really.

His questions turned to the subject of the dagger. "Where did it come from exactly?"

"I'm not sure, *exactly*... One of his lady friends, no doubt – a token of undying love from some married gentlewoman or other."

"Why have you kept it all this time?"

"Oh, it comes in useful." It really was dark here. We seemed to be the only two people out at this late hour.

"It can be used, then? It's a real knife, I mean, not just an ornament?"

"Oh no, it's perfectly serviceable," I assured him. "Here, let me show you."

With one fluid movement, I drew the knife from my belt, stepped in towards him and drove it deep into his belly, my free hand covering his mouth. In the dim light I could barely make out the look of disbelief and shock that froze his features. He had just started a low gasping moan when I drew the blade across his throat, silencing him forever.

He would have fallen then but for my supporting arm. I lowered him to rest in a sitting position against the wall. A quick glance round to make sure no one had seen anything, then I slipped a hand into his coat and relieved him of the bulging purse which had caught my attention when he first bought me a drink.

"You didn't stand a chance," I told his sightless eyes. "If not me, it would have been someone else." In truth, it was a miracle he had survived this long. His sort of naïvety came with a very short shelf-life.

I pocketed the purse, which felt satisfyingly heavy, then cleaned and did the same with the knife. "Sorry kid, but there's not much work around for retired heroes these days and I have to make a living somehow."

I stood, composed myself and strolled away, humming a half-remembered tune that Jimmy the Minstrel used to play around the camp fire. Gerard would invariably lead the singing with gusto. He had a decent voice, come to think of it.

Those were the days.

Two:
The Fisherman's Daughter

I left Cullen Ford the same night. Nobody there knew me – apart from the lad, and he wasn't about to blab to anyone – but, come morning or whenever the body was discovered, someone might recall us drinking together at the Golden Bear, particularly if my rugged features remained on hand to jog their memory. Best to keep one step ahead of any trouble by slipping away quietly.

The lad's purse yielded as much coin as it had promised – a welcome bolster to dwindling funds – but I was under no illusion regarding how long that would last, and travelling from town to town leaving a trail of slit throats and cut purses in my wake did not a career path make. I was bound to run out of either towns or luck at some point.

No, I needed to secure more reliable employment – no matter what its shade of honesty might be – and there were few opportunities to do so in this arse end of nowhere. It was time for me to return to civilisation.

Having decided on that much, I chose to head for the coast – which had always been the plan, or at least a vague notion.

Don't get me wrong, I'm not much of a sailor – give me firm land beneath my feet and a sword hilt in my hand over a pitching deck and a fistful of soggy rope any day – but you know the old adage: where there's a port there's commerce, where there's commerce there are merchants, where there are merchants there's mischief, and where there's mischief there's always the need of a good sword arm.

I followed the river to begin with, the Ayle, which had nothing to do with hops or fermentation, more's the pity. The name evidently derived from a word meaning 'arrival of spring' in a language nobody spoke any more. The track – it was too slight at this stage to be dignified with the term 'road' – led through idyllic woodland. The gentle rustle of leaves disturbed by the breeze, the chatter of birds, the occasional mournful cry of a solitary raptor sailing on splayed wings high above the canopy – it was enough to sooth the soul and cause a person to feel at one with nature. It might almost inspire a man to believe for a fleeting moment in Treemeisters – those benevolent overseers of the wilderness depicted in folklore as custodians of the wild places – but I was not such a man.

Nor was I entirely in the right frame of mind to bask in solitude and be lulled by the tranquil surroundings. I couldn't shake the feeling that someone was watching me. If so, however, they were very good at their job. I tried every trick in the book – swiftly dismounting after turning a blind bend and leading my horse off the track and into concealment to see who rode past, stopping at an elevated vantage point that offered a good view of my back trail and waiting, abruptly doubling back and pushing my steed into a gallop to surprise anyone who might be tailing me… Nothing. No one. Zilch.

Eventually I had to conclude that the only thing shadowing me was my conscience, and I could live with that; we hadn't been on speaking terms in many a long year.

The only blemish in this rural idyll was the occasional reminder of humanity's presence – here a single isolated hovel and, an hour or so later, there a cluster of two or three modest homes – nothing large enough to constitute a village or trouble the map makers but an intrusion none the less. At one point I passed two dour-faced men who sat huddled in a peculiar round boat in the very centre of the river. It was is if they sat in a bowl and their craft looked about as safe and stable as a drunkard trying to keep his footing on a frozen lake. I assumed they were fishing, but the thought did cross my mind that this might instead be an example of local justice and they had been banished there as some form of perverse punishment for crimes unknown. I didn't trouble to hail them to find out and they, in turn, ignored me.

It was still summer, if late in the season, and the evenings fell gradually, the sun's sinking below the treeline heralding a fading of daylight rather than an abrupt plummet. With the process well underway but not yet complete, I came across a fisher family's croft: a solid wood-built home situated up a steep bank and set back a little from the water, perhaps bearing testament to spring floods.

In exchange for a meagre amount of coin, I was able to secure a bed for the night and an evening meal. Weather conditions were clement enough that I could readily have slept outside under the stars, but even the prettiest of woodlands can change character after dark, when the nightshift arrives and nocturnal creatures emerge from their dens. I still hadn't shaken off the sense of being followed. I would rather have the added barrier of a wall – however flimsy – between me and any curious predator that might come snuffling, human or otherwise.

The family welcomed me to their table for the meal – which proved to be a thin fish stew flavoured with wild garlic, accompanied by unidentifiable but mostly softened tubers. I sat with the fisherman and his wife and their daughter around a roughly hewn and polished wooden oblong of a table.

The wife was a homely woman with a brusque attitude, while the daughter, Crista – a little plump-faced but certainly pleasant looking – caught my eye straight away, but so did the gutting knives hanging on the wall behind her father's hunched form. To judge by the furtive glances she favoured me with over dinner and the way she coloured prettily on the rare occasions I addressed her, Crista seemed quite taken with me, though I took little credit for that; it was likely an indication of how rare visitors were here as opposed to any wit or charm I was able to muster.

Unfortunately, the glares her father cast in my direction left little doubt that he had fathomed every thought that crossed my mind; his daughter's as well for that matter. He didn't actually say 'over my dead body' but his attitude implied as much. Normally I might have taken up the unspoken challenge, but not this evening. All I sought was a roof over my head and an undisturbed night's sleep.

Well, one out of two isn't bad, I suppose.

A long day in the saddle must have tired me more than I had realised. I normally consider myself a light sleeper and take pride in my reactions, but they let me down on this occasion.

My 'bed' for the night was the floor of the single room that comprised the building's downstairs, while the family retreated up a ladder to the loft area – evidently their customary sleeping arrangements. It wouldn't have surprised me had they pulled the ladder up after them, but they didn't.

For bedding they left me with a little fresh straw and a single sheet, which I lay on top of to prevent the straw from prickling too much. It was warm enough that I slept naked, pulling my jerkin over me as token covering.

The room was pitch dark – the single window shuttered and the lamps having been extinguished – and I soon succumbed to the enticement of deep sleep.

She must have moved stealthily, presumably familiar with the room's layout even in the dark. I didn't come awake until she was almost upon me. Not for a moment did I question that this was a 'she', that it was Crista; some subtle clue must have alerted me at the subconscious level despite the total darkness – perhaps a hint of feminine scent.

As I started awake, she shushed me wordlessly with a finger to my lips. I didn't feel threatened, confident from the start that she meant me no harm. My jerkin lifted slightly and I lay unmoving at her touch, as her hand glided down my stomach until she found my stiffening manhood, her fingers wrapping around it.

Her hands were surprisingly rough-skinned, a stark reminder that in this sort of environment everyone was expected to pull their weight, working to support the family even from a young age. The deft way she handled and caressed me suggested that this wasn't the first time she had done this, despite her evident youth. I wondered how many other travellers might have stopped here and been treated similarly...

In very short order I was fully erect, at which time I felt my jerkin pulled away completely and was conscious of her shifting position, straddling me. She gripped my shaft to hold it steady and lowered herself, engulfing me completely.

I let out a quiet sigh – it had been a while.

Instinctively, I reached out to grasp her hips but she must have anticipated the move, her hands gripping my wrists and pinning them to the floor. It was clear that she wanted to do all the work, and I was happy to oblige. She started to move, rise and fall, grinding herself against me. I thrust upwards with my hips, keen to match her rhythm, until finally our movements fell into an approximate semblance of synchronicity. There was no sound apart from her breathing, which grew more ragged and urgent, as did her gyrations. I wondered how long she could keep this up – in my mind it had become a sort of race: would my performance outlast her stamina?

In the end it proved a close run thing. I reached the point of no return far more swiftly than I care to admit – did I mention it had been a while? At least I could console myself with the knowledge that she beat me to it, just; her body trembling, her breathing becoming a rapid pant, nails digging into my wrist as her grip tightened – there and elsewhere – which is what pushed me over the edge and prompted my own fulfilment.

For a moment we stayed there, spent, her breathing now long and deep. I felt myself soften and slip out of her, then her weight lifted and my hands were suddenly released as she climbed off me.

Neither of us had spoken a single word. Tiny sounds traced her passage as she crossed to the ladder and ascended it again.

As quickly as that she was gone, leaving me to reflect on the encounter, which swiftly took on a semblance of the surreal, causing me to wonder if it had happened at all or whether I had merely dreamed the whole thing.

The next morning, Crista proved herself the consummate actress, giving no indication of what had passed between us during the night, even in unguarded moments when her parents' attention was elsewhere. So convincing was she that I might almost have fancied the whole incident a dream after all, were it not for the mild sting of shallow scratches that marked the inside of both my wrists, where fingernails had dug a fraction too deeply during the throes of passion.

I determined to take my leave early, keen to make as much distance as possible in the coming day. The fisherman and his daughter saw me off, while his wife – whose name I can't recall – busied herself in the background, tidying away.

I shook the fisherman's hand and, perhaps determined to generate some sort of reaction, lifted Crista's to my lips to kiss its back. As I did so, I paused – long enough that I was conscious of her father's stare and felt the need to explain myself.

"Sorry, I'm just marvelling at how soft your daughter's hands are," I said.

Crista coloured prettily at the compliment.

Having completed the brush of lips to skin, I released her fingers and straightened, looking past Crista as I did so to where her mother continued with her chores. For an instant she glanced my way and our eyes met. She didn't smile but I fancied there might have been a twinkle somewhere deep within.

Setting forth without further delay, I banished the fisherman and his family from my thoughts, consigning them to my past, where so many others have come to dwell.

Three:
The Inn of the Fallen Stag

The Ayle and I parted company somewhere around mid-morning. The river was destined to reach the sea eventually but would take its own sweet time in doing so, meandering lazily through the lowlands, and my needs were too pressing to pander to its whims; besides, a little further downstream there waited a town I felt obliged to avoid for a good while yet.

The water's course led through a gorge, and my chosen path rose steeply from the off; so much so that in a few places I was forced to dismount and lead my horse, though the beast was at least as sure footed as I could ever hope to be. It looked at me balefully, as if to reproach such a lack of trust. In truth, it was not so much his capacity to pick a suitable path I doubted as my own ability to cling to his back while he did so.

As a result, progress was slow in the short term but, if my bearings were right, somewhere over this hill lay a more travelled road that would lead me directly to Port Cray – a place I knew well if not recently. Cray was a bustling seaport, a veritable melting pot, where local merchants and others from more exotic climes were ever vying for advantage and opportunity. Two major families effectively ruled the town, controlling much of the trade. The heads of these two households held lofty opinion of their own worth, styling themselves 'the Merchant Princes'. Despite their pre-eminence, plenty of opportunities remained for others to operate in their shadow. Competition was fierce and it wasn't rare for rival interests to resort to violence when necessary. If I couldn't find employment at Cray, I might as well hang up my sword and return to the river to join those fellows in their circular boat and take up fishing.

I would love to claim that after a period of steady climbing my steed brought me to the summit of the hill, where I was able to pause and look back, contemplating the picturesque vista of a wooded valley through which the Ayle flowed serenely, its surface sparkling in the sunlight. Sadly, the truth was far more prosaic: the river's course soon disappeared from sight behind the treetops, while every time I hoped we might have reached the hill's crest it proved to be no more than a cruel tease, merely a fold in the landscape beyond which another slope still waited to be mastered.

As we climbed higher, the nature of the trees started to change. They grew squatter, their crowns lower and the spread of their boughs broader. Nor were these the only differences. Before long they adopted a rather singular form of adornment. Draped from every branch – or so it seemed – were veils of silken webbing, as if the whole woodland had been wrapped and bundled up in preparation for storage but then set to one side and forgotten about, left in plain sight for the whole world to marvel at.

A spider wood. Had I realised this was here I would have delayed leaving the river and chosen a different course. These places always gave me the creeps.

I recall my first encounter with a spider wood. As a boy I'd been enchanted, imagining this to be the home of fairies who sought to ward their realm in a vast wall of gossamer thread to keep the rest of the world at bay. Only later did I learn of the far more sinister giant arachnoids said to be the true masters of such places. Oddly, I had yet to meet anyone who had actually *seen* one of these malevolent creatures. No one worthy of giving credence to, at any rate; plenty of folk who claimed to know the second cousin of a woman whose best friend's brother once met a man who swore blind that he had fought his way free of a spider wood ahead of a pack of blood-crazed sharp-fanged monstrosities, barely escaping with their life... and the odd rascal professing personal knowledge of the mysterious realms that lay behind the webbing veils – invariably such individuals were in possession of both a vivid imagination and a raging thirst – but no one remotely convincing.

There was tell of a village somewhere in the north, near Hartbury if memory serves, that had been built in the shadow of a spider wood. Some local lord took it into his head that deep within that impenetrable cluster of trees there rested a great trove of treasure, jealously guarded by the woodland's eight-legged denizens in much the same way a dragon might covet its hoard. So obsessed was he with this notion that he worked tirelessly to convince others, filling their heads with dreams of wealth. Soon he had all the villagers believing the tale. One fine summer's day, fired up by his seductive fancies and undoubtedly fuelled by too much sour mead and scrumpy, they determined to flush out the wood's custodians and seize the treasure for themselves.

Urged on by their lord, the villagers had set light to the woodland. Now this was following a period of protracted drought, so the trees and the brush all caught readily. The villagers watched and laughed and drank, anticipating their imminent wealth, but fire is a capricious ally, reluctant to follow direction, and the flames soon rampaged out of control, spreading like, well... wild fire. Before the villagers knew it, the conflagration threatened to engulf their very homes.

Drawing water from wells at both ends of the small settlement, they did their best, flinging bucket after bucket at the flames, but they might as well have tried to douse a dragon's breath by spitting.

Finally the fire burnt out, but not before it had consumed the entire woodland, the village, their meagre attempts at agriculture, and much of the wild grassland beyond. Those responsible never saw any giant spiders – concluding that any such must have perished in the flames – nor did they find any treasure, just a vast swathe of blackened earth. All that remained to indicate where their homes had once stood were a few charred splinters of stunted wall.

With their homes gone, no hunting to be had and no crops to support them, the community disintegrated, the people drifting away to settle elsewhere, but almost at once shoots of green began to appear, as saplings emerged from the seared earth. In a surprisingly short time a green mantle of fresh growth had spread across the blackened land as the woodland started to renew itself. Most mysterious of all, as the trees grew ever taller with each passing season, the veils of webbing reappeared. Things had returned to their prior state, as if the fire and the villagers' foolishness had never been. The only significant change was that the woodland had now expanded slightly, reaching out to reclaim the land formerly occupied by the village.

The moral of the tale has always seemed pretty obvious to me: leave well enough alone. A principle I'm more than happy to abide by where spider woods are concerned.

We passed the long stretch of brooding trees without incident, though my sense of being watched had returned, stronger than ever, and this time it wasn't the prospect of human pursuit that made me jumpy.

As soon as the spider wood was behind us my spirits rose considerably, and I chided myself for succumbing to such irrational fears – I didn't believe in giant arachnids any more than I believed in Treemeisters or fairies. Such tales were for the young and the gullible, not a seasoned warrior such as I.

Not long after, I found myself under open sky, the woodland falling away entirely to leave me riding across terrain virtually devoid of trees – presumably too exposed or the soil too poor. A landscape of bare stone, brackens and grassland, where large rocks thrust forth from the earth in dramatic pose, as if caught partway through being expelled by some terrible cataclysm beneath the ground. For all I knew they might well have been at some point in the distant past – such matters have never numbered among my strong suits.

As I picked a course through these towering tors, I noted that several of them bore the scars of human attention, that here and there giant faces had been carved into the stone. Many of the details had been lost to the passing years, obscured by lichen and moss, whilst others had been badly weathered, their features so worn away by the elements that I struggled to discern them at all. If old Sirus were here, I'm sure he could have told me which ancient people were responsible for the sculpting, and would then have embarked on a protracted explanation regarding the significance of these ancient faces to this deity or that. Thankfully, it was many years since I'd been subjected to that form of abuse.

Although the land here undulated in a series of gentle rises and falls, I gained the impression that the overall trend was downward, and dared hope that I had indeed crested the top of the hill and was now well on my way to the road that memory promised.

I soon found myself riding among trees again, very definitely descending, if fitfully. By late afternoon I had reached level ground, more or less, and emerged from the treeline to find the road directly in front of me.

Unfortunately it was already occupied, by folk who didn't look any too keen on the prospect of sharing.

The sketchy path I had followed since leaving the river grew ever more ill-defined towards the end of its course, degenerating to the point where it was little more than a game trail. I was preoccupied with picking a way through thorny tangles and avoiding low-hanging boughs, concentrating more on where my steed was treading than on our surroundings, so it came as something of a surprise when the trees abruptly ended and we stepped out into the open, with the road suddenly revealed.

"Who the hell are you?"

I blinked, taking in the man who addressed me. "I could ask the same of you."

Only after I'd spoken did I register the presence of the two archers who flanked him, arrows nocked and pointed my way, not to mention the two further men who sat ahorse, one either side of me, with swords drawn and levelled.

"You could," he agreed, "but I'm betting you're not that stupid."

"Oh, I don't know," said the swordsman to my right. He was the oldest of their company – a veteran – which suggested a degree of competence, since the incompetent rarely lived to see his level of maturity, not in this game. "Judging by the amount of noise he made blundering around in those trees, if this is his idea of sneaking up on us he can't be none too bright."

Unless I'm merely the diversion, I thought, *a feint to distract your attention from the real attack.* For once my brain worked quicker than my mouth, and I suppressed the impulse to say this out loud, lest one of the archers took the comment seriously and decided to put an arrow through me, freeing them up to concentrate on whatever the real threat might be.

"I'm not sneaking up on anyone," I assured them instead, taking care to keep my hand well away from my sword hilt, "just taking a shortcut to get to the road, that's all."

"He was making more noise than a blinded hog let loose in a scullery," the veteran reminded the first man who had spoken – presumably the officer in charge. While focussing on him, I considered my options.

Just because the pair flanking the oficer sported bows didn't make them expert archers. The swordsman on my left was younger, much younger; he sat his horse nervously, the tip of his sword wavering as he struggled to control his mount, his unease inevitably transmitting to the beast which looked to be one loud noise away from bolting. He was the weak link and so would be the focus of my attack if matters came to that. It would take me away from the veteran but also leave my back exposed to him.

Not much I could do about the archers – moving swiftly and hunkering down as low in the saddle as I could might make their job a little harder, but most likely not enough – and what about the other two who hung back behind the commander and archers? They were evidently guarding a fancy-looking coach drawn by a team of impressively large horses. Undoubtedly this accounted for the party's aggressive reaction to my appearance.

All in all, I didn't rate my chances if it came to a scrap.

That left only one resource to fall back on: my charm, which has never been the most reliable of assets.

I smiled and raised my hands further away from my side and weapons, spreading fingers to emphasise that they were empty. "Look, I'm just on my way to Port Cray seeking employment. Last thing I want to do is pick a fight." *Not with the odds stacked against me like this, at any rate.*

"Where have you come from?" the commander asked.

"Cullen Ford," I replied, reckoning honesty to be the best policy, especially as no word of cut throats in back alleys could have spread this far this quickly.

"Took the river road and then cut cross country?" the veteran asked.

"Yes."

"It is the quickest route, Captain," he said, looking across at the officer.

The captain nodded and tension levels dropped palpably. The archers didn't lower their bows just yet but their shoulders relaxed a fraction and the veteran went so far as to drop his sword arm, the lad on my other side immediately following his lead. I felt able to breathe again.

"I'm going to be travelling in the same direction as you," I said, "but a good deal quicker." I nodded towards the carriage. "If you let me pass, I'll be on my way and we'll likely not have to see each other again."

"Very well," the captain said. "I'd rather have you in front where I can see you than at my back in any case."

His logic was difficult to fault. I eased my horse forward, the veteran keeping pace beside me, ensuring he stayed between me and the carriage.

I spared the coach an inquisitive glance in passing, wondering who it was these men guarded so zealously. There were windows but they were covered and I had yet to see anyone peering through to discover what all the fuss was about; perhaps it was no person at all inside but some*thing* rather than some*one*, the means of transport no more than an elaborate ruse to disguise the cargo's true nature.

It was a small coach, large enough to carry two in comparative comfort, perhaps more at a squeeze – I've no great love of coaches, finding them an uncomfortable mode of transport on the few occasions I've ridden in one. At least on horseback you can establish a rhythm, accommodating your mount's gait. In a carriage you are at the mercy of every bump and dip in the road, the jolting mitigated only marginally by cushioned seating.

This road was well travelled, the surface too compacted and solid to show any significant ruts behind the carriage, but I gained the impression that it was heavy. The team pulling it consisted of four Becconshires. Veritable giants of the horse world, Becconshires are muscle-bound powerhouses, any one of which could have pulled the coach on their own if it were empty. Four seemed an unnecessary extravagance if a mere person or two sat within.

The veteran stayed by my side until we were well past the party and on the open road.

"Fighting man are you?" he said casually.

"More often than not."

"Perhaps our paths will cross again in Cray." Was that a threat, or a warning, or no more than innocent comment? His tone offered no clue.

Since he was being chatty, I decided to push my luck in the hope of finding out more about the contents of the carriage. "I've worked escort more than once myself. Might I ask…?"

"No," he said, cutting across me. Not *that* chatty, then. "Safe journey."

With that, he turned his horse around and trotted back to the carriage and its guard.

The Inn of the Fallen Stag is a popular staging post for those on route to Port Cray, who frequently discover that the road is a fair bit longer than the daylight. Tempted though I was to ride on through the night, my horse was worn out and I was little better, aching in ways that I could swear never troubled me in younger years. Besides, the venison broth they served at the Inn was justifiably renowned and the lad from Trilmouth's purse remained reassuringly full. What's the point in having coin if you're not prepared to treat yourself every now and then?

The Inn and I were not complete strangers. I'd stayed here once before, some years back, on which occasion I made the mistake of saying "No" when the burly fellow behind the bar asked if I'd heard how the inn came by its name.

"It's an interesting story," he assured me.

It wasn't.

Forewarned is forearmed and this time, when an entirely different barkeep asked the same question of the man standing next to me, I snatched up my drink and beat a hasty retreat to a vacant table in the far corner of the room.

People-watching has long been second nature to me. Not because I find my fellow humans especially fascinating but for reasons of self-preservation. When you've made as many enemies as I have over the years, it pays to assess the lie of the land, to judge who has noted you and who hasn't. The bar was not especially crowded but there were enough folk present to keep the staff occupied. In such situations I tend to start by assuming that everyone around me poses a potential threat, and then consider each in turn, downgrading the level of risk they might pose as I go.

For the most part, the motley who had gathered in the Fallen Stag's taproom that evening seemed unremarkable in every way. There were the usual travelling tradesmen, more than a few professional men at arms such as myself, the occasional couple – though there were only a few women present and none were unaccompanied – the poor victim trapped at the bar who looked ever more desperate as the barkeep's dull tale plodded on, a Valkyrie of a barmaid moving between the tables collecting empties and exchanging lewd banter here and there – invariably getting the better of things, but then I suppose she'd had more practice. No tellers in evidence, for which I was grateful; I wasn't in the mood for a story that evening.

As mentioned, *for the most part* nobody looked out of place, but there was one notable exception: a group of four men huddled around a table a little away from me. They hunched protectively over ales that had been there since before I sat down and remained barely touched – props rather than anything intended to quench a thirst – and they looked alert while all around them were relaxed. They were trying hard not to watch the door and failing, clearly waiting for something or someone. Occasionally three of them would remember themselves and make some over-loud jest accompanied by a guffaw or an exaggerated back-slap, but these were isolated instances. One among their number never joined in these mimes. His attention remained focussed on the door, though his gaze skittered everywhere but.

Sometimes patience can bring its reward. I sipped at my own ale – making it last, not wishing to be distracted by a trip to the bar and miss whatever this group might be waiting on – and made a point of not overtly studying the four men, hopefully with more conviction than they were displaying. They paid me no mind, which suggested I succeeded.

Every time the door opened to admit a new arrival, as it did three or four times during the hour or so that followed, the quartet all glanced that way in unison, they couldn't help themselves, only to instantly resume their efforts to look disinterested when the wrong person entered.

Finally the moment came. This time when the door opened they tensed noticeably, and didn't relax when those responsible strode into the inn. I can't pretend that I was especially surprised to see half a dozen men come in, led by the veteran and the officer who had been so protective of the mysterious carriage. It made sense that they would stop here, after all. Their only options were to stop in the open somewhere close to the road – which would have necessitated guard rotations and dulled reactions the following day – ride through the night with all the hazards that entailed, or stop over at the Fallen Stag. The latter seemed far and away the safest course, especially given their zeal in protecting whoever or whatever it was they guarded, and the inn's beds were definitely the most comfortable option.

Ever since first setting eyes on my four twitchy friends I suspected this was who they were waiting for. After all, only something of value would warrant such patience, and whatever that coach contained it *had* to be valuable. The nature of its worth seemed common knowledge to everyone but me, a galling omission I had every intention of remedying.

The captain strode towards the bar, sweeping past me and evidently oblivious to my presence. The veteran spotted me, though. He scanned the taproom as soon as the party entered, and nodded when he saw me. There was neither warmth nor hostility in the gesture; it was simply acknowledgement. If he also noted the four hunched watchers he gave no sign, which was surprising and raised a whole new set of possibilities.

I studied the guard party where they clustered by the bar, noting that the youngest wasn't with them – suggesting that he had drawn the short straw and been assigned first watch, guarding the carriage or its contents. If the latter was indeed person or persons unknown, they must either have remained with the carriage or been smuggled in through a backdoor, because they certainly weren't in evidence here.

No sooner had the captain and his group reached the bar than my four twitchy friends rose from their seats and headed out the door. It didn't take a genius to work out where they were going. For a second longer I watched the guards gathered at the bar, debating how to proceed.

It seemed to me I had three options: one, do nothing and mind my own business; two, slip out discretely to observe whatever might unfold in the inn's rear courtyard from a safe distance; three, alert the captain and his squad to my suspicions. If you'd set me this as a theoretical conundrum and asked me which course I'd choose, I would have said option two every time, so quite why I acted as I did remains something of a mystery, even to me. Perhaps I sensed in the veteran a kindred spirit, or perhaps the obviously nervous youth who had held his sword towards me with hands that couldn't stop trembling had stirred a spark of compassion in my dark and twisted soul, reminding me of myself so many many moons ago; or maybe I simply saw this as an opportunity to ingratiate myself and so increase my chances of finding a job. Most likely it was a combination of all these things, with the prospect of employment tipping the scales. Whatever the motivation, I stood up and strode to the bar almost before I realised it.

"I think you may have a problem," I said to a startled captain and the veteran, who seemed to take my approach and my warning in his stride.

"Oh, how so?"

I watched their faces as I told them, and realised that my news was no news at all. With a nod from the captain, first to his men and then another to the barman, the entire party moved to a small door beside the bar, which the veteran pushed open, allowing them to file briskly through into the inn's private quarters. Of course I followed, how could I not? The familiarity demonstrated by all concerned left me in no doubt that there were more layers to these events than I'd suspected, and I wasn't about to miss seeing how things played out.

The men hurried through a dark hallway and into a scullery, gathering by a back door. Knowing I hadn't been invited to this particular party, I hung back. They waited, weapons drawn, the captain with one hand grasping the door latch. I couldn't see anything through the small window due to the press of bodies, but presumably someone could.

"Now!" yelled the veteran.

The captain threw the door open and led the charge. So eager were they, so animated, that it's a miracle everyone avoided impaling each other on their brandished swords in the press to get outside. I brought up the rear and so missed much of the action, but the details revealed themselves readily enough.

The anxious whickering of horses disturbed the evening, and there came a loud thump, as of a heavy hoof striking against wood. The sun had set, daylight fading though not yet entirely gone. Directly opposite us, the twin doors of the stable had been flung open. Revealed in the half-light by flickering torches, the coach stood within the stable, though it was barely recognisable as the carriage the captain and his men had been escorting. It appeared to be missing one entire side, that nearest us, which had evidently dropped to the ground on hinges. Finally I got to see what occupied the interior: three men at arms, currently in the process of discarding crossbows and jumping or clambering down from their vantage point.

Between us and them were three figures I recognised from the inn; two were down, crossbow quarrels protruding from their torsos. One lay unmoving, the other was on his knees, groping at the bolt as if trying to decide what to do about it. As I watched, he keeled over, the decision no longer relevant. The third figure remained on his feet, apparently uninjured but looking around as if he couldn't quite grasp what had befallen him, let alone how to react. The sight of our party erupting from the back of the inn did the trick. He flung his sword aside, thrust his empty hands towards the stars and dropped to his knees, shouting, "Please, don't... I'm unarmed!"

Having arrived a little late to the party, the captain and his men looked disappointed, as if they'd been hoping to get in on the action. Not that I could blame them. Several days spent riding a bland road, trudging along at a snail's pace to stay with the carriage, only to have the bowmen claim the glory when the monotony finally lifted: it would be enough to make any man despondent.

Ever since I stepped out of the inn and took in the scene, I'd been searching the margins, scanning the edges of that patch of light cast by the torches in an effort to find the fourth man, the least twitchy of the group from the taproom. He was missing, having avoided the fate of his companions. Presumably he had hung back to see how things developed, ready to make good his escape and report to his masters whatever the outcome...

Finally I saw him, over to my left, skulking in the shadows as anticipated. What I *hadn't* anticipated was that he held a crossbow of his own, which must have been secreted out here some time earlier because it hadn't been in evidence in the taproom. The captain had closed the distance to the surviving ruffian, making it difficult to tell which of them might be the skulker's intended target, but it certainly looked to be one or the other.

I didn't hesitate, reaching behind my back to draw one of the set of throwing knives I habitually carried there. The man was a considerable distance away and the light wasn't good. Despite the absence of a wind this was a difficult throw, impossible for most men.

I'm not most men.

I strained with every sinew, putting my full body weight behind the cast, and watched the blade fly true. Perhaps I grunted, or perhaps the veteran caught my movement in the corner of his eye. He shouted a warning, presumably an instinctive one before appreciating where my knife was aimed. Too late, in any case. The blade struck home. The skulker dropped his bow, the shot never made, and collapsed to the ground.

Alerted by the veteran's call, the captain looked round – too late to see the blade strike the man, but in time to see his body hit the ground. Startled, he looked from the skulker, to me, to the veteran and back.

I strode forward while everyone hesitated. Doing my best to appear unhurried, confident and in control of the situation, I crossed behind the captain and his men to where the skulker's body lay. My movement broke the tableau.

"Bind this man," the captain said, indicating the survivor, and his men hurried to obey.

Having retrieved my knife and wiped it clean on the dead man's clothing, I sheathed it behind my shoulder and glanced across to find the captain watching me. He nodded, perhaps in thanks, certainly in respect.

I responded in kind and then headed back into the inn and the taproom, leaving the captain and his men to organise the clear up. The veteran clearly had similar thoughts and was a few steps behind me.

"Impressive throw," he said as we stood together at the bar. "Can't think when I've seen better."

Not being one for false modest, I didn't reply, instead saying, "Your carriage is a decoy."

"Obviously."

"So what was supposed to be in there?"

"A priest."

"A *priest?*" I'd been contemplating a number of possibilities, but not that one. "A devout man, is he, your employer?"

"Not especially. More a desperate one."

He clammed up after that, perhaps fearing he'd said too much, and stepped back from the bar to claim a vacant table. I followed and, when he didn't object, sat down opposite him, not asking any more questions, suspecting that the truth regarding this elaborate deception would emerge soon enough.

"If it's a job you're wanting, you did yourself no harm back there," he assured me. "The captain'll be grateful."

"He seems a bit…" I hesitated to say what I was really thinking.

"Green?" The veteran had found a far politer turn of phrase than I'd been considering. "Yeah," he continued, "he's that all right. He's also the boss' nephew, which is how he comes to be captain."

"And you've been tasked with keeping an eye on him and making sure he doesn't mess up," I guessed.

He grunted. "That, and keeping him alive."

I didn't envy him. Playing nursemaid to a dull-knife is no one's idea of fun. "Good luck with that," I said. "Guess this means that *you* owe me too, then." I grinned in the face of his scowl.

The captain joined us soon after, insisting on replenishing our ales. Well, it would have been rude to refuse.

That evening I was at my most charming, building on the advantage gained by my earlier heroics and giving them every reason to trust me. Clearly I played the part well enough, because when I asked, "So what was all that about back there?" the captain took me into his confidence.

"There are two big players in Cray," he explained, leaning in and talking quietly so as not to be overheard.

"The Merchant Princes," I said, hoping to forestall a detailed lecture on things I was already familiar with.

"There are countless other trading families and consortiums," the captain said, "but the Merchant Princes are the only two that really matter. They hold the *real* balance of power, and our employer is the greater of the two. We work for House Brystone."

So much for hope.

I'd never heard either of the two Houses described as being 'greater' than the other, but it emerged that their noble employer had suffered a series of setbacks of late, constantly losing out to their bitter rival, House Storm. In an effort to reverse this trend, the current Prince Brystone had secured, at considerable expense, a ring set with a fire stone – an incredibly rare form of gemstone which was said to bestow good fortune upon its owner.

"So where does the priest fit in?" I asked.

"In order to maximise the stone's influence, it has to be blessed by a Priest of Scarl," the captain explained.

"Really?" I'd heard the legend of the fire stones, of course, but had never before come across that particular piece of nonsense. Though, given my lack of interest in quaint myths about good luck trinkets, that was hardly surprising.

"Turns out these bloody priests are even rarer than the fire stones," the veteran muttered. "We've had to smuggle one in all the way from Yarlow."

"So you let it be known that this priest would be travelling to Cray in the heavily guarded coach out there while spiriting him in by some other means," I said.

"That's about the size of it, yeah," the veteran confirmed.

"Was it worth it?"

"How'd you mean?"

"So you've just killed three hire-swords and captured a fourth." I shrugged. "An operation like this must have cost House Brystone far more that it cost House Storm to hire those men, so was it worth it?"

"Of course it was," the captain snapped. "We bloodied their noses, and captured one of their agents to boot…"

"A hire sword who will not be part of House Storm's usual retinue and whom they'll deny all knowledge of," I pointed out.

"Maybe, but people will still know…" the captain insisted. "We've shown them that the tide is turning. Storm has lost face, that's what counts."

And there was me thinking that all that ever really counts for a merchant is the coin, but who was I to argue?

The veteran chose to keep his own counsel, and after this exchange the conversation took a lighter turn. The captain relaxed considerably as the evening drew on, and it became apparent that he was a happy drunk rather than a maudlin one.

Feeling that I had played my hand admirably and ingratiated myself sufficiently for one evening, I decided to take my leave and head for bed. As I went to do so, the captain said, "I've always liked this place." His gaze took in the tap room and the whole of the inn. "Remind me to tell you someday how it came by its name. Fascinating story."

"I look forward to it," I said, frozen smile firmly in place.

Four:
The Prince and the Priest

We all have a past; the trick lies in not allowing it to shape your future – a lesson I've struggled with over the years. Having a reputation can do that. Human nature has much in common with water flowing down a hill, in that it will always seek the easiest path, which is what makes the temptation to constantly rely on my rep so hard to resist. For example, when trying to secure a potentially lucrative job, which hire-swords are circling like vultures at a fresh kill, I *know* that being associated with Gerard and his celebrated band will give me an advantage – but there's a downside to this as well. It also gives me something to live up to, and that's where I tend to fall short. I'm much better at living down to things these days.

Returning to Cray felt different. Following my heroics of the previous evening the captain had invited me to join House Brystone's guards – an appointment that would need to be ratified by the Prince himself, but he insisted this was merely a formality. So I rode into town with my back straight and head held high. For once a job had come my way without the need to fall back on my past, and that pleased me more than it probably should have; it felt good to know that I was about to start work for a Merchant Prince purely on my own merit. The prisoner, my ticket to this success, was firmly secured and on display for all to see – House Storm would know of their failure before we'd even dismounted.

We entered the town a few days before Founders' Day, and I doubted the timing was coincidence, the Prince almost certainly planned to show off the fire stone at the ceremony, to the envy of his rivals.

We approached Port Cray via the main road across Denton Moor. Viewing the city from this vantage brought back many memories. From here the town looked to be a crowded mass of rooftops which sloped precipitously down towards the sea, as if the buildings were sliding that way and the only thing preventing them from spilling into the ocean and disappearing beneath the waves, row by ragged row, was the harbour with its barrier of blocky warehouses and tall-masted ships. Perspective can play tricks on the mind, and the houses looked to be so tightly packed that I could imagine a giant might have scooped them up, enfolding them in its outstretched arms and squeezing them together before placing them back on the ground. Only as you drew closer did the huddled mass of tile and wall draw apart slightly, revealing itself to consist of distinct buildings; only then did you realise with any certainty that there *were* streets here, albeit narrow and twisty ones. Memory assured me that there were broader and more direct avenues in the town as well – including two that gave access to and from the harbour for goods and personnel and a third that bisected these two – but none of them were apparent from here.

As we came nearer still, an aspect of Cray I had done my damnedest to forget made its presence known: the smell; an odd odour that strove to be fish-like but didn't quite make it, tempered as it was by all the less pleasant perfumes generated by such a concentration of humanity. The result was a unique cocktail which I could have identified as 'Port Cray' with my eyes closed. Fortunately, experience had taught me that in a comparatively short while your nose grows accustomed to the stench – either that or it rebels in horror and refuses to acknowledge it any longer.

We didn't need to venture into the centre of town, instead skirting its outer reaches, crossing to where a sprawling manse squatted within walled grounds: High Balvue, the ancestral seat of

House Brystone. I had passed the place any number of times during my previous time in Cray without ever setting foot beyond the walls. It was therefore with a strange mix of curiosity and unease that I rode through the opened gateway in the wake of the carriage; unease because I couldn't escape a vague sense that in doing so I was blithely stepping into a trap – being within an enclosed compound tends to have that effect on me, a legacy of my time in jail.

On this occasion, though, I had a feeling there was more to the general sense of disquiet that pervaded the place than echoes of my past. Something here wasn't right.

The captain and veteran went straight to see the Prince to deliver their report, making no mention of anything amiss. Being the new boy, I was tasked with stabling the horses alongside the lad who had held a trembling blade to me when I first encountered the party. Jorge he introduced himself as – clearly mistaking me for someone who gave a damn. He seemed oblivious to any problem at High Balvue and his ability to talk proved a worthy counterpoint to my reticence. As a result, I could readily have learnt his family's complete history in all its mundane glory during the brief period that followed, had I been of a mind to pay attention. I suspect he was angling to set me up with his sister, judging by the way the monologue was going, but fortunately the captain returned to whisk me away before the full extent of Jorge's intentions were laid bare.

"The Prince wants to see you," the captain said.

I couldn't much have cared who wanted to see me at that juncture, just so long as it took me away from the vicinity of the stables. It did surprise me, though, that it was the captain of the guard who came to fetch me rather than one of his men, suggesting that his authority was even more cosmetic than I'd appreciated.

"Prince Brystone likes to vet all new members of staff, no matter what else is going on," he explained. "Nothing to worry about – he'll take my recommendation, but he prides himself on the personal touch." Further evidence that either the Prince saw himself as a 'hands on' commander or that he lacked confidence in his lieutenants. I filed the possibility away for future reference. "This will likely be the briefest of audiences in any case," the captain continued, "given the current state of turmoil."

Turmoil? I suppose such things are relative. Even allowing for my vague sense of unease, all about us appeared calm, at least on the surface. If this was turmoil, I'd hate to see the place when nothing was afoot.

"Why turmoil?" I ventured. After all, no one's going to dangle a piece of information like that unless they want you to ask.

"It's the ring, the one containing the fire stone," he explained. "It's been stolen." He reported this with a degree of excitement that suggested he relished such intrigues. "Nothing else taken, and there was no break-in, it just disappeared."

"An inside job, then," I observed – I'm as capable of stating the obvious as the next man.

"It must be. Spirited away by one of the Prince's own staff. He's livid. Everyone who was here is being interviewed. We'll get to the bottom of it, mark my words."

So the Prince formerly had a fire stone but no priest to bless it, and now he had a priest but no fire stone to be blessed. Somehow I managed not to laugh, though it was a close run thing. A smile must have escaped, however, which the captain noticed.

"This is no laughing matter," he snapped, belatedly remembering his station.

"Of course not," I agreed, keeping my face deadpan.

We continued in silence after that. He led me briskly across an open courtyard which boasted some spectacular plants – bright orange flowers the shape of trumpets, their petals vivid enough to rival the finest sunset, and other smaller blooms that were white shot through with purple, like jewels hidden beneath the snow – and then through a series of regally dressed corridors, with an ornately carved chair tucked in a corner here and a marble bust on fluted plinth there. A single long tapestry adorned the wall of one such, stretching the full length of the corridor and depicting, or so I gathered, one man's life: progressing from apple orchards in childhood, a hooded hawk in adolescence, through a battle or two interspersed by what might have been marriage, a castle, and the arrival of children, then another battle and finally what looked to be a peaceful end in bed, with doting family in attendance. I had no idea who this might have been, but the tapestry was a masterpiece and must have taken the artisans responsible years to complete.

The next corridor bore a number of portraits in heavy gilt frames, which I surmised were past Princes of House Brystone. A young lad ran past us as we neared the far corner, heading in the opposite direction – first hint of the 'turmoil' the captain had mentioned.

All this I glimpsed in passing, the captain setting a pace that suggested the current Prince didn't like to be kept waiting. Either that or he was frightened of missing something if he stayed away for too long.

The house seemed to be built around a series of small walled gardens, with every corridor offering views of one or other through the windows in one long wall, while the other wall contained closed doors for the most part – always of polished dark wood. It was a veritable maze in honeycomb form. Some of the courtyards had guards stationed in them, others did not. I could discern no logic in the system, and quickly gave up the attempt.

Eventually we arrived at a pair of imposing arched doors – dark wood like the rest but taller and intricately carved with the impression of leaves and climbing vines. Unlike every other door we'd passed, these stood at the end of a corridor rather than to the side, which conveyed a sense that this was the point to which every route through the house's labyrinthine interior must eventually lead.

Two guards were stationed here. At our approach they swung the great doors open and for the first time I entered the presence of a Merchant Prince. And at last I caught a proper glimpse of the 'turmoil' the captain had warned me about. The Prince was on his feet, shouting at two guardsmen. The veteran stood to one side, as if ready to assist or offer counsel if required: the sort of position I would have expected a captain to occupy. There were several other guards present, though all seemed to be doing their best to sink back into the walls, in hope of avoiding their employer's attention. Evidently dismissed, the two berated troopers left the room, hurrying past us with eyes downcast.

Wonderful; summoned into the presence of my new employer just as he seemed hell-bent on biting someone's head off. All of a sudden Jorge and his clumsy matchmaking didn't seem so bad after all.

The Prince flung himself down into a chair and glowered. He still hadn't acknowledged us, which was fine by me. If not for the captain standing so resolute at my side, I could probably have sidled out quietly... Denied that escape, I took the opportunity to study this head of a merchant dynasty instead.

He was younger than I'd anticipated, and thinner, slighter in every sense – in fact he looked decidedly unhealthy. Somehow I always expected the privileged to be... Well, to be candid: mature, well-nourished, distinguished-looking or even corpulent, depending on their willpower, and in rude health. Of course, I knew the title of 'Merchant Prince' was hereditary, so the incumbent could be pretty much any age, but this man didn't fit my preconceptions in the least, an impression not helped by the tantrum he'd been throwing as we entered. It made him seem petulant, and diminished somehow.

The Prince was seated upon a surprisingly plain chair, although deeply cushioned and raised upon a low dais – as if to suggest that he was royal yet remained humble. Standing before him, revealed now that the two guards had been dismissed, was a slight figure who could only be the Scarlene Priest, or rather

Priestess, for this was clearly a she. Robed in white and hooded, I had yet to get a proper look at her face, but by her build she could be little more than a youth.

The captain cleared his throat, drawing the Prince's attention. "Yes!" he snapped.

"My Lord Prince Mycal of House Brystone, may I present..."

At that precise moment the priestess turned her face fully towards me, and suddenly everything else in the room fell away. I was incapable of contemplating anything beyond her.

Julia.

Just a quick look and then she faced forward again. I'd missed the captain's final words and now he had finished speaking. All eyes were on me – apart from the priestess', that is. I suddenly realised I had no idea how to behave. Should I bow? In the absence of any prior instruction, I settled for a quick bob of the head.

"Noble Prince," I improvised, "it is an honour to serve the renowned House of Brystone. I pledge my sword to your service for as long as you'll have me." *And for as long as you pay me*, I added in my head.

The Prince waved a dismissive hand and mumbled a few distracted platitudes before dismissing me. I couldn't resist a further glance towards the cowled priestess on the way out, but she made no effort to look my way again.

They put me to work immediately. I was tasked with guarding one of the small courtyards – open to the sky but boxed in on all four sides by walls and windows. I still had no idea *why* it required guarding – perhaps to prevent thieves from making off with one of the prettily flowered shrubs or the single slatted wooden seat – and standing sentry was not exactly what I'd envisioned when signing up, but this hardly seemed the appropriate moment to complain, and at least it provided an opportunity to clear my head.

This time it was the veteran who showed me to my post rather than the captain. "Best place to be at the moment," he said. "Keep your head down while the Prince decides what he's gonna do about House Storm."

"It was definitely House Storm, then, who stole the fire stone?" I said.

"Of course." He eyed me thoughtfully. "Unless, that is, you know different."

I shook my head quickly, though I could think of at least one other candidate.

It didn't take long to assess my surroundings once the veteran had left me. At the centre of the courtyard stood an oddly posed marble statue: an androgynous individual – who, after much consideration, I concluded was most likely a young woman – balanced on one leg and tipping forward as if she were either skating or in the process of falling over. The carving was exquisitely rendered by a skilled hand, suggesting that both the androgyny and the peculiar stance were deliberate, though I couldn't for the life of me fathom the significance. Not that I was particularly intrigued, you understand, but there was little else to contemplate at the time.

Doubtless the lack of available distractions accounted for where my thoughts inevitably turned: Julia. The last time our paths had crossed she'd been in the company of that batty old coot Sirus – a colleague from my days with Gerard. I had found her beguiling and had been strangely infatuated with her, which she later explained away by claiming that Sirus had placed a charm on me to ensure my assistance in their venture. Fine as far as it went, except that being a practical man I didn't believe in glamours and charms, and if that was all it amounted to, why did her face continue to haunt me some two years later?

I heard a noise behind me – nothing overt, just a whisper of foot on stone – the sort of sound someone might accidentally make if attempting to creep up on you. I spun around, knife in hand, taking a hasty step backwards to put distance between myself and whatever the threat might be.

It was her. Of course it was her.

"Relax." She held up empty hands. "If I'd wanted to kill you, I'd have done so without letting you know I was here."

Letting me know... Right.

After the briefest of hesitations, I slipped the knife back in its sheath.

"Thank you for not giving me away in there," she said, taking a step closer.

I gazed at her face – remembered so often – not quite able to believe I was seeing it in the flesh again: the bright over-large eyes, the small mouth, the delicate features that had caused me to wonder more than once if there might be some elven blood in her, a natural beauty only slightly marred by the scar – less vivid than I recalled – which ran from the corner of her left eye to the centre of her top lip.

The white robes of priesthood were gone, replaced by more familiar and closer-fitting black, or rather charcoal grey; never true black, which stands out in shadow rather than blending into it, despite what some might have you believe.

I stood my ground but didn't move forward as I would have done to greet an old friend. Were we? Old friends, I mean. To be honest I had no idea.

"It seems that we've both wasted our time," she said. "Assuming, that is, you're here for the same reason I am."

It would have been redundant to ask what that reason might be – a thief tricking her way into a household which had recently acquired a rare and very precious gemstone...? So instead I shook my head. "I just came to Cray seeking employment."

She laughed. "Of course you did. It's pure coincidence, you happening to show up right now."

"As a matter of fact... *yes*, it is."

I could tell she didn't believe me – why should she? Before she could press me further, I asked a question of my own. "So it's not your doing then, the fire stone disappearing?"

"I wish. No, it was gone before I arrived, just. Had I been a day or two earlier…"

"And what became of the real Scarlene Priestess?"

She shrugged. "As far as I know, there aren't any, at least not any more."

That gave me pause. To make a switch and take someone else's place was one thing; to establish a false identity as a priestess from scratch, solid enough to be accepted by someone who came looking, quite another. The latter required considerable planning and preparation, which spoke of an elaborate scam rather than one hastily put together to take advantage of an opportunity. "Who are you working for?" I asked.

She grinned. "Sharp as ever." The smile fell away almost as soon as it formed. "Some very dangerous people, the sort I really wouldn't want to disappoint. The ring being stolen… complicates things."

I could see how it might.

"We need to get it back, and quickly," she added.

"Hang on, 'we'? Who is this *we* you speak of?"

She took another step closer, until we were nearly touching. I could smell her; a feminine, almost floral scent that might be fitting for a priestess but seemed incongruous on the Julia I knew. The air between us felt electric, and my breath quickened as I gazed down into those deep brown eyes.

"You and me, of course. I did save your life, after all." She spoke the words softly, seductively.

They weren't a lie as such, merely a gross over-simplification, one which conveniently ignored the pivotal role I'd played in a hazardous job successfully undertaken on her behalf. I couldn't deny, however, that she did help me reach safety afterwards when I was sorely wounded, and had then been on hand to watch over me while I healed.

That was two years ago. We hadn't seen each other since, despite my keeping eyes and ears open for any word of a small but deadly thief who could pass for an innocent youth. Not that I'd been looking, you understand, just… curious.

I swallowed, finding my mouth unaccountably dry. "Seems to me that what you really need for a job like this is a thief," I said. "One skilled enough to hug every scrap of shadow, becoming almost invisible and slipping past guards like a ghost – perhaps even someone with Nightblade training."

"Oh, very droll."

"If the hat fits…"

She stepped back, enabling me to draw a much-needed breath. "I would go, of course, but I can't. I'd be missed, my absence impossible to explain. It was an expensive operation running decoys and bringing this Priestess of Scarl to Cray, even for a Merchant Prince, and Brystone won't risk losing both me *and* the ring to his rival. I'm under constant guard – just slipping away for these few minutes has been a challenge, even for me. So my hands are tied. I need someone I can rely on to do this for me, someone I can trust. I know first-hand how capable you are, and… There's no one else. I need you."

Suddenly the distance between us disappeared and she was pressing against my chest, snuggling. "Please. Some dangerous people have invested heavily in this venture. If I fail to deliver the stone, they'll kill me. You wouldn't want that, would you? And you *do* owe me."

Refusing someone has never been more difficult. I pulled away, shaking my head and turning my back on her, hoping she would interpret the actions as internal debate. "The thing is," I said, "I've only just arrived here, only just secured a job with one of the Merchant Princes. If I desert to pursue a personal mission and *don't* bring back the ring, you know how that'll look. Even if the Prince doesn't kill me out of hand, he has enough influence to make sure I never work in this town again." *And there are already too many towns where I daren't show my face.*

"Sorry, but…" I looked back over my shoulder to make sure she understood, only to discover I was alone. I hadn't heard her go.

I was still mulling over the conversation an hour later when a far bulkier figure entered the courtyard: the captain.

"The Prince wants to see you again," he said.

Despite my own inner turmoil, I managed to refrain from passing comment on his status as errand boy; even I have standards.

I couldn't help but wonder, though, as he led the way back through the mansion's corridors, who would be guarding the courtyard in my absence. After all, if it had been worth guarding in the first place, why hadn't the captain turned up with someone to relieve me? Unless, of course, these guard posts dotted around the complex served no real strategic purpose whatsoever but existed primarily to impress any visitors, while giving otherwise idle soldiers something to do.

The Prince occupied the same seat as he had before. A second chair had been placed on the dais beside his, angled so that it faced partially towards him while still taking in the rest of the room. The positioning subtly conveyed that whoever sat there was subordinate to him despite being privileged. Julia was that person, once more robed in white priestly gowns.

The pair regarded me as I entered in the captain's wake, and I felt that for the first time I actually had the Prince's attention. Not a wholly comfortable feeling for someone of my dubious pedigree, but I endured his gaze without flinching.

The silence stretched into long seconds, as he evidently weighed up what he saw.

"I've been hearing good things about you," he said at length.

Of course he had. Neither the captain nor the veteran had anything to gain from downplaying my actions, as that would only have highlighted their own failings. I wondered fleetingly what had happened to the prisoner. No one had mentioned him since our return and I suspected he had outlived his usefulness.

"As you may have heard, a precious item has been stolen from me. I need to get it back." I didn't much care for the way this was headed. "I'm told you're the man for the job."

"*Me*, noble Prince?"

I studiously avoided looking at Julia, concerned that if I did so the fury might show on my face. Trust her to come up with a way of getting what she wanted while turning my own words against me. Where now my argument for not helping her because I didn't want to desert my post? Thanks to her manipulation, it *was* my post.

"Indeed. You are new to my service, so unknown to my enemies and less likely to draw suspicion." And no doubt easier to disavow if things went wrong, as they surely would: I was a warrior, not a sneak thief, unlike someone I could mention. "Fear not," he continued. "I don't expect you to embark on such a vital mission alone." Of course he didn't, not when there was a chance I might succeed and then run off with the stone myself.

"So I am sending my worthy Captain of the Guard to accompany you." Oh great; a dull-knife who needed a nurse maid even when he was in command. How could we possibly fail? "He is relatively new to this house himself, and is unlikely to have drawn anyone's attention." The captain tensed beside me at the thinly veiled insult, but kept his own counsel.

"Captain Gerard, I charge you with ensuring that the ring is returned safely to me."

Gerard? I realised this was the first time I had actually heard the captain's name.

"Yes, my Prince!" he said.

I was still struggling to process this revelation. Not an uncommon name perhaps, but even so… It was enough to make a man believe in gods – the perverse sort, those who take delight in the cruellest of jests at the expense of their mortal subjects.

Gerard.

Five:
House Storm and the Fire Stone

It was a suicide mission, anyone could see that. House Storm would be expecting Brystone to make a play for the ring, and what better time than Founders' Day, when every official of note and every merchant worth the name gathered to celebrate the port's official birthday?

Over the years Founders' Day had developed into a form of competition, a declaration of status in which every attendee would strive to demonstrate their superiority over some rival or other: who could muster the most men at arms arrayed in the most elaborate ceremonial uniforms being one of the most significant indicators. Storm would *have* to show up in force or lose face, but that didn't mean their House would be left unprotected, it just meant they would hire more swords.

In the two days since the Prince had tasked me with recovering the fire stone, I'd had a chance to assess the captain's metal. What I saw came as a pleasant surprise. Mind you, bearing in mind how low my expectations were to begin with, that would not have been difficult. His earnest approach and eagerness were commendable, however, and given two or three months I might have made a half decent soldier out of him. Sadly, all I had was two days.

On the morning of the mission, we donned House Storm ceremonial surcoats and token armour. The armourer supplying the garments guaranteed they was authentic and 'this year's livery'. Easy for him to say: it wasn't his life that would depend on the accuracy.

The captain had pitched up with a crossbow. I stopped him as soon as I saw it.

"Are you an expert with that thing?" I asked, indicating the bow.

"No, but I can…"

"Then leave it."

I found it amusing how radically the dynamic between us had shifted. From the first moment of training it was apparent that I was by far the better swordsman, the more experienced warrior, and wilier fighter. Without anything being said, he had steadily come to rely on me for advice and direction, deferring to me despite his nominal status as the 'officer'. That switch of roles continued even now and would do, I suspected, at least until the mission was over. However that might pan out.

"Unless you're an expert, that contraption is as big a threat to us as it is to our enemy," I said in the face of his confusion. "In a close fight it'll either hinder you and most likely get you killed, or you'll be forced to abandon it to free your hands, so why bother lugging it around in the first place? How were you thinking of concealing it, eh?" I had him on the ropes and wasn't about to let up. "Besides, the bow is a coward's weapon, a sneaky way to kill. A good honest blade, that's what we'll rely on." I tapped the pommel of my sword for emphasis.

His mouth opened and closed without actually speaking, as he strove to find a counter argument but failed to do so. Instead, he set aside the bow, with obvious reluctance but without further protest.

Shortly after, the two of us slipped out of High Balvue via the servants' entrance, swaddled in heavy cloaks to conceal our vestments. It wasn't the hottest of days but nor was it the coldest. The cloaks soon had us sweltering and, I'm sure, made us the shiftiest-looking individuals abroad that day. Rarely have I been more pleased to shed a piece of attire, which we were finally able to do in a narrow back alley. Here we met with a man also dressed in House Storm livery; the only difference being that he was being paid to wear it. Of course, he was also being paid considerably more to betray it. I always feel uneasy around turncoats. It's so hard to tell at what point they chose to stop turning. As someone whose moral compass is often swayed by weight of gold, I'm loath to trust anyone who manifests similar principles.

The veteran had spoken highly of him, though, declaring this to be one of his 'best men'. The judgement of others is something else I struggle with, preferring to rely on my own assessment.

For his part, the turncoat seemed no happier to be a part of this venture than I was to have him. "This caper of yours had better work out," he muttered. "I can never go back to House Storm after this."

"You're being well rewarded," the captain pointed out, with the sort of authoritative snap that I hadn't heard in his voice for a while. "You managed to get away without arousing suspicion?"

"Yeah," the turncoat assured him. "I feigned illness on the way to the square as planned. Made myself throw up at the side of the road and was sent home – they seemed to think I wouldn't bring much credit to the House if I vomited over some dignitary in the middle of the ceremony."

After a quick inspection of our own disguises, which the turncoat endorsed with a resounding "You'll do," we set off. It was a relief to be walking openly once more, unhampered by the cloak.

House Storm was a very different sort of building to High Balvue. The two powerhouses of Cray claimed opposing hillsides, glowering at each other across the valley occupied by the town. Whereas Balvue was a bloated manse that sprawled over a large area of land but stood just two storeys high, Storm resembled a castle rather than a house. Compact rather than sprawling, its sombre walls rose to four storeys, more if you counted the turrets that anchored each corner; all in all, an edifice built to impress, which successfully dominated the surrounding area.

Our gaining entrance relied on the fact that so many additional men had been hired to cover both the deployment for Founders' Day and security at the House. The hope was that the guards on the door would recognise Turncoat and accept his two appropriately dressed companions, even if they didn't specifically recognise our faces.

That part at least went like a dream.

"Her Ladyship sent us back to collect a necklace she meant to wear today," Turncoat told the two guards while we hung a little way back.

"You mean she changed her mind again," one of them said.

"Not for me to say."

"Wouldn't want to be in the maid's shoes," the other guard added. "It'll be her fault, no doubt, whether she's even heard of the necklace or not."

They waved us through without a second glance. To his credit, Turncoat had held his nerve admirably.

I still didn't trust him.

Once inside we moved at a brisk pace – none of us had any reason to linger. I was struck by how dark the interior of this place was compared to High Balvue. I'm sure one wasn't built deliberately to be the antithesis of the other, but they might as well have been.

Turncoat led the way along a high-ceilinged corridor whose windows were too few and too small, and then up a broad flight of stairs that split partway. Confronting us as we reached the landing where the stairway divided and doubled back, were a trio of portraits in gilded frames, each depicting a severe and haughty-looking individual. These ancestral portraits were pretty much interchangeable with any of the similar daubings that hung on the walls of High Balvue, as far as I could see.

Without sparing the paintings a second glance, Turncoat took us up the left-hand stairwell. At the top he turned right, moving at the same assured pace he'd adopted throughout – a man on a mission. I liked that: such a show of confidence, that air of 'I belong here and will brook no delay' had carried me unchallenged past many a potential obstacle in the past.

Unfortunately, not this one.

"Where the hell do you think you're going?"

The speaker, a veritable mountain of a man, stepped across to block our way. He stood directly before the ornately carved door which Turncoat was clearly leading us to.

"Move aside! Turncoat snapped. "I'm here on her Ladyship's business."

"Is that so?" The guard eyed him up and down, feet still firmly rooted to the floor.

"Her Ladyship requires me to fetch a necklace which she had intended to wear for Founders' Day but has left in her rooms, and she wants it ten minutes ago." His no nonsense tone almost convinced *me*; I had to admit that Turncoat was proving his worth.

"You're not part of her Ladyship's retinue," the guard said.

"Of course I'm not! Her Ladyship's personal retinue are still by her side, where they belong. I'm just the bloody messenger boy sent back to pick up a necklace."

"And what does that make these two?" Man Mountain allowed his gaze to slide across the captain and me, evidently unimpressed by what he saw. He still gave no indication of being persuaded by Turncoat's words.

"I didn't say it was a *cheap* necklace. They're here for added security, obviously."

"Well, be that as it may, my instructions are clear. Only her Ladyship or members of her retinue may enter these rooms. You'll have to go back to the Prince's party and return with…"

I'd heard enough. His words trailed off as my throwing knife sank into his left eye.

Mountain or not, he was still human. There was just time for a semblance of shock to form on his features before he collapsed with an impressive thud, a vibration felt through the soles of my feet as much as heard.

"What in the name of the seven gods have you done?" Turncoat stared aghast, first at me and then at the dead guard.

"Removed an obstacle."

"But did you have to *kill* him?"

"Yes," I said, crouching to retrieve my knife. "Your words were getting us nowhere and time is pressing. The longer we're here, the greater the risk of discovery and so of failure."

"But this is the Prince's champion, the captain of House Storm's guards…"

"Was," I corrected him.

The captain of House Brystone's guards stared down at his fallen counterpart. "Wasn't that sneaky?" he asked me.

"What?"

"You said earlier that you didn't like bows because they were sneaky. Isn't killing someone by throwing a dagger at them much the same thing as killing them with a bow and arrow?"

I stared at him for a split second, trying to find the words. If he couldn't see the difference between granting someone a noble death with a good clean blade and the ignominy of plucking their life away with the pointy end of a feathered stick, what hope was there?

In the end I settled for an exasperated shake of my head. "Come on, give me a hand with this." I reached out to grab the dead man's ankles.

The guard proved just as heavy as he looked, but between the two of us we managed to drag him quickly into the private rooms while Turncoat kept watch, anxiously looking this way and that to make sure nobody had seen us. Mind you, if they *had*, goodness knows what he would have done about it.

A slight smear of blood remained on the floor, but there wasn't much we could do about that, and a smear is far less conspicuous that a hulking great body.

Turncoat came in to join me and we shut the door, leaving the captain in the hallway to take the sentry's place. I would have preferred to have Turncoat out there – a familiar face – but I needed him in here since he was the only one of us who knew where the ring was supposed to be. It was a risk, but any guard was better than no guard at all and if things went to plan we wouldn't be in here for long. We could only hope that no one passed this way in the meantime or that anyone who did saw the uniform and not the face.

I've been in many an opulent room in my time but suspect her Ladyship's may number among the most impressive. Much lighter and airier than the other parts of House Storm I'd seen, it benefitted from large windows and what looked to be a small balcony beyond. The four poster bed was predictable, as were the frescos on the panelled walls – pastel scenes of open countryside and clear blue skies – but to be honest I was a little too preoccupied to pay the decor much heed.

"You're sure it's in here?" I asked for the dozenth time, still not quite able to believe the Prince hadn't chosen to lock the fire stone away in a fortified basement room with a squad of guards stationed around it.

"Yes, I told you," Turncoat said, "her Ladyship insisted, and then *pleaded*, and there's little the Prince can deny her when she turns those big brown eyes on him."

"So he just left the ring here, in her quarters, with a single guard."

"He could hardly have taken it to Founders' Day with him, could he? 'Oh look, House Brystone, here's that ring I stole from you.' There'd have been a bloodbath. Besides, it wasn't just *any* guard he entrusted its safekeeping to, but the greatest warrior in all of Cray."

I glanced over to where the body lay just inside the door. "If you say so."

Despite admitting that he'd never set foot in these rooms before, Turncoat knew exactly where to look, leading me to an over-elaborate dressing table dominated by a large mirror and decorated with flamboyantly carved scrolls of white-painted wood. "Maid told me," he explained. "While describing in detail how one day she was going to fund her future by stealing all of her Ladyship's jewellery before sailing away from Cray forever."

"Never harms to have a dream," I said, attempting to prise open the locked drawer he'd indicated, which was proving to be stubborn. I paused to push aside a heavily padded chair which hadn't really been in the way but was annoying me, and then applied the knife blade again. This time I was rewarded, as the locking mechanism gave way with an audible snap and the drawer sprang open.

All manner of sparkly things were revealed within, each neatly arrayed and carefully housed in its proper place – a bracelet that seemed to consist entirely of square-cut blood red ruby's strung together in four rows, the largest pearl drop pendant I'd ever seen, a gold locket edged with a circle of small diamonds, a broach of filigree silver strands surrounding an impressive emerald – one face of the stone sitting proud of the filigree web – diamond rings that must have cost the equivalent of a year or two's wage for the entire household…

I hesitated. This was all too easy.

Turncoat showed no such restraint. "Now isn't that a sight for sore eyes?" he murmured. "Her Ladyship's finest trinkets, all laid out just asking to be plucked. Can't tell you how long I've dreamed of laying my hands on these."

"No wait…" I moved to grab his arm but I was too late. He reached inside, his fingers closing on the ruby bracelet.

Even as they did so, a thin blade arced out from the lining of the drawer in a blur of steel, slicing neatly across the inside of his wrist, severing blood vessels. At the same instant, twin needles like a snake's fangs sprang downward from the top of the drawer to puncture the top of his hand.

With a shriek, Turncoat dropped the bracelet and snatched his hand away, reaching with his other hand to grab a cloth from the top of dresser, spilling perfume bottles and a dainty silver vinaigrette in the process. He clasped the cloth, which looked to be silk and so was hardly the most absorbent of bandages, to his wound, seeking to staunch the flow of blood though with little success.

His gaze sought mine, beseeching, but all I could do was look on helplessly.

"Do someth…" The word trailed off in a brief hiss as his eyes rolled upward, his head jerked back and his knees gave way. He collapsed to the floor, sinking down in rapid stages like a marionette with its strings cut. Blood spread rapidly from his outstretched wrist to pool around his lifeless hand.

Using the tip of my knife I turned the hand over, doing so gingerly, to expose the puncture wounds on the back. A tracery of jagged black lines ran from each mark, like fractures in glass, and the skin around the holes already looked unhealthy, necrotic. I drew my blade back hastily, glad I hadn't touched that dead skin with my own; whatever poison had been employed here, it was fast acting and not something to be messed with.

Turncoat had fallen foul of two booby traps, either one of which would likely have done for him. I suspected they were designed to work independently and only the crudeness of his actions had triggered both simultaneously, which didn't mean there weren't more.

Taking my knife, I eased its blade into the gaping maw of the drawer, careful to keep my hand outside.

Nothing. By keeping the blade in the centre of the space, no defences were triggered, but all that changed the moment I brought it forward, towards the front of the drawer. Once again the thin blade swept out in an arc, clashing with my knife. I suspected that had my movement been upwards towards the roof of the drawer the metallic fangs would have come into play. Ready for it this time, I was able to observe and appreciate the elegance of the mechanism, if not the precise method of its action.

Taking out a second knife, I inserted the two blades in opposite corners of the drawer, pointing them downwards, and used them to pull it further open, hoping to take the needles out of the equation by doing so. Keeping the knives in the corners also avoided triggering the swinging blade, and soon the drawer gaped wide.

Towards the centre and hidden from view until that moment sat a row of a dozen or more rings, there bands sunk into a slotted cushion and their gems facing upwards. There was no mistaking the one I was here for, despite my never having seen a fire stone before. Among the array of diamonds and other precious gems this one stood out. For its simplicity as much as anything else. The stone was deepest amber in colour, cut in a round multi-faceted style and mounted on a gold band that was a little thicker and flatter than any of those around it. There were no embellishments, no smaller stones surrounding the fire stone to set it off, just this one dark orange solitaire.

I nearly reached inside to claim it but still didn't trust that drawer, even though two booby traps were surely enough for most circumstances. Again I resorted to my knives. Choosing a long stiletto, I carefully reached in to dislodge the ring, using the blade's tip to lift it clear. I held my breath as the ring came free, but nothing happened, no new surprises leapt out to threaten me.

I drew the blade out and seconds later the ring nestled in my palm. It felt disappointingly mundane, not warm or cold to the touch, not fizzing with mysterious energy, just a ring. Now that the fire stone had been secured I was free to contemplate the rest of the drawer's contents. I mean, nobody had said that I *couldn't* help myself to anything else, and this seemed too good an opportunity to refuse. Emboldened by my recent success, I employed the stiletto with confidence, electing to lift out the multi-rowed ruby bracelet that had been Turncoat's downfall first and then a gold necklace that had been beside it, before setting about the remaining rings, collecting each of them in rapid succession. The swinging blade and the needles were old news, easily avoided, and they proved to be the only defences the drawer had to offer.

If circumstances had allowed, I would have cleaned out the rest of the contents in a matter of minutes, but the sound of raised voices from beyond the door brought me up short. *Damn!* I had dallied too long and left the captain exposed in the hallway.

Tucking away my knife, I abandoned the drawer and its remaining temptations, stepped over Turncoat's body, and hurried across to the door. Even before I reached it, the nature of the commotion beyond had changed, the volume and agitation of the voices rising and then being replaced by the unmistakeable sound of steel meeting steel. The captain had clearly been identified as an imposter – a ruse that was never likely to survive close examination – and was being forced to fight.

My sword was already in my hand but I hesitated, undecided how best to proceed. There was no way of telling how many of House Storm's guards the captain faced, and my flinging the door wide and charging out to join the fray in reckless abandon struck me as an invitation for disaster. On the other hand, delaying until they had dispatched the captain and came in here after me would give them the opportunity to summon reinforcements, and that could leave me facing a small army with no support or allies.

In the end it was no choice at all. Cursing whatever gods had brought me to this point, I wrenched the door open and threw myself into the hall, a dive that became a forward roll, sword still clutched in my right hand. It was a manoeuvre I'd used once or twice before, prompted by desperation and promising myself on each occasion 'never again'. This time, feeling my shoulder blade protest and something pull in my side, I meant it. Bloody stupid idea.

It worked, though. A sword sliced through the air above me as I rolled, a blow that would have landed somewhere around waist height had I been standing. I came to my feet, my hastily raised blade parrying a strike from a second assailant, half-numbing my upper arm since I hadn't had the opportunity to set myself properly.

I sprang backwards, in part to give my arm a few seconds to recover but mostly to assess the situation. There were three of them. The captain had taken a wound to his left side but was still holding his own against one of them. I had to trust he could continue to do so, however hard pressed he might be, because that left me facing the other two. One stepped in towards me, while the other took a step to the left, away from my sword arm. Decent enough tactics, though the narrowness of the hall hampered them. I feinted to shuffle backwards – a move they might have expected of me to avoid being outflanked – but instead leapt forward, taking the offensive, which they were less likely to anticipate.

A lunge followed by a sweeping cut, both of which t man before me parried, but the combination drove him back. Then I was forced into a parry of my own as the second guard attacked, but at least the resultant manoeuvring left them both in front of me.

I switched my sword from right to left hand, lunging at left-most of the two whilst also stepping sideways to ensure his body remained between me and the first guard, preventing them from both engaging me at once. At the same time, I pulled out a knife and threw it right-handed at my opponent. This wasn't a throwing knife and the cast was improvised and clumsy, but that didn't matter. He batted the knife away as anticipated, but in doing so left his side exposed. I drove my sword home, taking him below the right arm, a little above the cutaway in the inadequate breastplate.

Pulling my sword free of his collapsing body, I swapped it back to my stronger right hand and advanced on the other guard. Within half a dozen rapid exchanges I had his measure. We both knew by then that I was the better swordsman and I watched desperation dawn in his eyes as he realised there was nothing he could do about it. Two, three more parries and my blade slipped past his guard, running him through.

I turned in time to see the captain's legs buckle. He still managed to parry a heavy blow as he dropped to his knees, but it was clear that his strength had failed and the next strike would do for him.

It never fell. His opponent made a mistake that marked him a sadist. Rather than finishing the job as rapidly as possible, he hesitated for a second, as if determined to give his victim time to appreciate the inevitability of their fate; the pause wasn't long: a heartbeat or two, but it gave me the opportunity to close and skewer him from behind. Had he been more clinical, I would have been too late.

"They saw the smear of blood... on the floor," the captain explained, his chest heaving.

"Save your breath." I helped him to his feet, impressed despite myself; with only a few days' proper training he had held his own against three guards and then kept one of the trio occupied long enough for me to dispatch the other two. Unfortunately, his wound looked serious and there was a lot of blood – what was I saying about only a few days training?

"Fire," he croaked.

"What?"

"Fire!"

At first I thought the pain was making him delusional, then I realised what he referred to. Smoke. I'd been so focused on the fight that I hadn't noticed anything else, but now the violence had ended I could pay more attention to our surroundings. Tendrils of grey floated along below the ceiling, the smell of it acrid in my nostrils, whilst my eyes were smarting. Somewhere not too far away, House Storm was aflame. Happy coincidence, or did the veteran have another agent within the rival Prince's service, now acting to cover our incursion?

I could hear running feet, too, and voices raising the alarm.

"Come on." I helped the captain to his feet. "Can you walk?"

"Yeah, I think so."

I helped him anyway, my shoulder under his good arm, my hand wrapped around his waist, trying to ignore the sticky damp warmth gathering beneath my fingers.

The smoke grew thicker as we retraced our steps, heading back to the split staircase Turncoat had brought us up. Here we had to pause as a squad of guards rushed past, heading upwards. I half expected a challenge but they paid us no heed, focused on dealing with the fire. However, a black-suited footman in their wake paused long enough to say, "There's a nurse in the lower scullery, ready to treat anyone hurt."

I thanked him and wondered, as he hurried after the guards, whether later he would find time to recall the nature of my companion's wound and ponder.

Progress down the stairs was a lot slower than I would have liked, with the captain's strength noticeably ebbing. If I didn't get him to a medic soon, he wasn't going to make it. Despite that, at no point did I consider seeking out the scullery and the promised medical help there. If he survived but did so in the keeping of Prince Storm, Brystone's guilt would be proven, the House's reputation tarnished beyond repair. So instead we pressed on, along the dingy corridor that led to the only exit I knew, but with the front door just around the next corner, I could sense that his legs were going.

"Just need to rest a moment," he gasped, trying to sit down.

"No!" I hissed. "We're almost there. A few more minutes and we'll be home free. Then we'll get you straight to a medic."

As we rounded the corner my heart slumped. A guard stood there, though he hadn't seen us yet. I thought him to be one of the two who had been standing sentry outside the door when we arrived, and guessed that the two had been brought in by the threat of the fire, one going to help their comrades fight it while the other remained at his post. I had hoped they might both have been summoned away.

The captain saw the guard too, and asked, "Now what do we do?"

"Distract him," I said.

"How?"

"Like this."

I punched the captain in his wound. Predictably, he screamed. Already alert, the guard by the door spun our way, straining to see what was happening.

"Over here," I yelled. "I've got one of them."

To his credit, the sentry didn't desert his post immediately but hesitated, clearly undecided. "One of who?"

In the nine names of Hell, hadn't they worked out what was going on yet?

"One of the thieves!" I yelled at him. "The fire's just a distraction. Caught this one making a break for it. Come on, man! I can't hold him forever." I prodded the captain's wound again, eliciting an agonised yelp.

That did it, and the guard came sprinting over.

"You bastard... What... what are you... doing...?" The captain was gripping my arm, sobbing and panting with pain, his whole torso heaving with the effort to breathe.

"Sorry," I whispered, "but with a name like 'Gerard' there was only one way this was ever going to end." I already had a knife out and plunged it into his back, thrusting upwards to pierce whatever organs it met, all out of sight of the approaching guard. The sobbing and the panting ceased, just as the guard arrived.

I took in his uniform at a glance. It was the same ceremonial get-up that all the House Storm guards were wearing today, including me: token breastplate, helmet with cheek guards, but no chainmail beneath it, nothing to protect the throat.

I allowed the captain's lifeless body to drop to the floor and stepped forward to stab the knife that had ended him into the guard's neck, giving him no chance to react or even to realise what was going on. He gave voice to a strange sound somewhere between a wheeze and a gurgle. Then he wilted, pulling free of my blade as he went down.

I didn't hesitate but ran hard, and was halfway across the floor before his body came to rest. Wrenching the door open, I flung myself through, glad to be out of that grim place. The day welcomed me with cool air, and from across the street the deep dark shadows of an alleyway beckoned.

Six:
The Shattering of Dreams

The plan was to return to High Balvue as swiftly as possible while skirting around the centre of town – I didn't want to risk bumping into House Storm's Prince and Lady or a contingent of their guards on the way back from the Founders' Day celebrations. Barely had the walls of House Storm fallen behind me, however, when I blundered into the veteran in company with Jorge, the young lad from the coach escort.

"We've been waiting for you," the veteran explained, "keeping an eye on House Storm to help cover your escape in the event you might need it."

And to make sure I didn't 'escape' in the wrong direction taking the fire stone with me, no doubt.

"Guessed you'd come this way or close to it," he continued. "It's quick, but not the most obvious route. Just glad you weren't much longer – it's a pain in the arse skulking around places we've no excuse to be." His gaze flicked up to look beyond me. "The captain?"

"Didn't make it."

"My agent?"

I shook my head. "Sorry."

He grunted. "Well, that'll save the Prince one substantial pay out at any rate. Did you succeed...?"

I fished out the ring and showed it to him, careful not to reveal any of the other jewellery in the process. His eyes lingered on the stone, and for a moment I thought he was going to order me to hand it over into his keeping, which could have been awkward: I had no intention of doing so whatever the consequence. It had been my life on the line back there, not his.

He made no such demand, though, instead simply nodding and saying, "A job well done. Now keep it out of sight," before turning to lead the way back to High Balvue.

There was no fanfare to greet us. The Prince was absent, having not yet returned from Founders' Day, and the bulk of the House's guards were with him. It felt odd, coming back to High Balvue at such a time, like entering a building that had been deserted in a hurry – the recent occupants having left clues to their residence in the signs of everyday living that remained, while they themselves were absent. There were still guards at the main door, but those sentries previously positioned randomly in corridors and courtyards were nowhere to be seen. Unlike House Storm, Brystone hadn't hired any extra men, not really having reason to do so.

Julia was still present, or so I was informed. I didn't see her, but instead found myself closeted in an antechamber awaiting the Prince's return, the fire stone ring still in my possession. Both the veteran and Jorge stood by the door; part guard, part warden, I suspected. They were friendly enough but made it clear I wasn't going anywhere.

Word of my return and most likely of the mission's success must have reached Julia by this point, and I pictured her demanding to see me without delay, attempting to persuade those guarding her with mounting desperation. If she could get here, claim the ring and be out the house before the Prince and his retinue returned, she could lose herself in the backstreets and alleyways of Cray. She had always been streetwise, and I'd back her to make a clean getaway if she got that far, for all this was the Merchant Princes' town.

She didn't appear, though, suggesting that her guards were as resolute as my own.

Thankfully, I didn't have to wait long before being summoned. Founders' Day must have been drawing to a close even before I escaped from Storm, and we clearly didn't beat the Prince back to High Balvue by much.

There were guards aplenty now, as if to emphasise the Prince's return, standing sentry at their eccentrically determined posts as if they had never been away: normal routines resuming after the disruptions of the day.

This time, at least Julia looked up as I entered, though I wasn't under any illusion regarding where her real interest lay.

"You have the fire stone?" It was the Prince who spoke rather than the priestess.

I nodded, and produced the ring, holding it out towards him. He didn't take it, though, gesturing me to give it to Julia instead, which I did. She sat beside him as she had when I was last here, and didn't meet my gaze, having eyes only for the ring as I placed it in her open palm. A small wooden table stood before her, on which rested a jeweller's eyeglass and an elegantly wrought silver hammer, its long handle curved to mimic a swan's neck, the hammerhead seeming to blossom out of the handle rather than being fixed to it, as if the two had been forged from a single ingot.

She picked up the eyeglass, pushing back her hood in order to bring the loupe up to her right eye. In her left hand she held the ring, bringing it almost reverently up to study.

"Fire stones are the rarest and most precious of all gemstones." She spoke softly, her words undoubtedly meant for the Prince but I couldn't escape the sense that she was speaking directly to me as well. I hadn't retreated since handing over the ring and nobody had told me to, so wrapped up were they in the moment.

"There have only ever been twelve in all the world, did you know that?" Julia continued. "Many of those have been lost to us – part of vanished treasure troves or gathered within private collections and then forgotten about when the collector died, the heir failing to recognise the jewel's significance. It is always a special moment when one of the lost stones surfaces, as perhaps we have here." She turned the ring slowly between her fingers, staring at it intently, studying each facet of the amber jewel.

I had to hand it to Julia, she must have done her research – it seemed unlikely she was winging this performance – and what a performance it was! I knew full well that before me sat a talented thief and con artist rather than a learned Scarlene Priest, but she inhabited the role so thoroughly that even I was starting to wonder if there might be more secrets hidden in her past than she had admitted to. No; it wasn't possible. I knew she had once been a member of the notorious Nightblades; how did a misspent youth running with a cadre of anarchic assassins square with apprentice priesthood in an obscure ancient religion? It didn't.

This was an act, plain and simple. Albeit a highly accomplished one.

"In truth," she continued, "only one large fire stone has ever been unearthed, and the location of the mine that spawned it remains a closely guarded secret." She spoke so softly that I had to lean forward, straining to catch her words. A quick glance around told me that everyone present, even the Prince, was doing the same.

"All twelve of the stones I spoke of were cut from that single large gem and set by a master craftsman within identical rings. Each stone is unique, though to the unschooled eye they appear to be the same. Only a Scarlene Priest is taught to discern the subtle variations, but those variations are key, for they define the nature of the gift that each stone bestows upon its owner."

"Nature of the gift…?" the Prince said. "I thought fire stones are supposed to bring luck and good fortune."

"They do indeed," Julia confirmed. "But each stone influences a different aspect of fortune, bringing luck in different forms."

"I had no idea."

"There's no reason why you should. Legend and rumour are never the most reliable of informants, and when they are your only guide…" Suddenly she paused. "Ah."

"What is it?"

She didn't answer, but calmly took the loupe away from her eye and placed it on the table. The ring she put down beside it, before sitting back straighter in her chair.

"You've identified it, then," the Prince said, a little too eagerly. "You can tell me the nature of the good fortune the stone will bring to both myself and to House Brystone?"

"Oh yes, I can tell you exactly the nature of this stone's influence." She moved swiftly, her hand a blur which my mind registered only in after-image as she snatched up the slender hammer and brought it down onto the gem with a resounding crack. The fire stone shattered into myriad pieces.

"None whatsoever," she said into the shocked silence that followed.

"In the name of all the Gods!" The Prince roared the words as he started to his feet. The veteran reached for his sword, more by reflex than with any intent to draw, I think.

"Twelve stones there are, twelve facets of a greater whole," Julia said, her raised voice cutting through the moment, calmness personified in the eye of the storm she'd created. "But this is not one of them."

"Explain yourself, priest, or know my wrath," the Prince said, regaining some of his poise but not his temper.

"I'm sorry, my Prince," Julia said, bowing her head in deference. "Truly I am, but your fire stone was a fake, a cunning forgery cut from glass to mimic the genuine stone."

"But I had it examined by experts…"

"No, my Prince, you did not, not until now. When it comes to fire stones there *are* no experts outside of the Scarlene priesthood. This was a fine piece of work, fashioned by a skilled craftsman with deception in mind. I had my suspicions at first sight of it, when I first *heard* of it. More than half a century has passed since one of the lost stones came to light. My suspicions strengthened when I failed to identify your stone. Regrettably, this little demonstration has confirmed my worst fears. No true fire stone would ever shatter at such a simple kiss of steel, whereas glass…" and she gestured toward the table with its explosion of shards and glassy flecks. "Will."

I found the veteran at the Tapered Eel – an inn with a bit more class than most and an establishment I'd been told he enjoyed. It wasn't far from the House, either, which was another thing in its favour: less distance to stagger.

That morning, the one following Founders' Day and everything that had transpired, found me back on sentry duty in the same small courtyard. I spent long joyous minutes examining the surroundings to see if anything had changed in my absence but failing to find such.

Light relief arrived in the form of an unexpected visitor; the same unexpected visitor as last time, though on this occasion the meeting was official and so more formal. It was the Scarlene Priest rather than the thief/assassin who graced me with her presence, dressed in full robe and hood of her office. Two guards accompanied her, though they remained at a respectful distance as she came across to me. The long robe hid her feet and created the illusion that she was gliding across the paving rather than walking.

She held out her hand, permitting me to hold her fingers as I bowed to kiss it.

"Before I go," she said, "I wanted to thank you in person for all your efforts and your bravery."

"You're leaving?"

"Yes, I depart within the hour. With the fire stone having been revealed as a fake, there's nothing to keep me here and I must return to my duties in Yarlow."

"Of course." *What duties?* "Then I bid you safe journey."

Not once during the exchange did her mask slip. Not once would anyone have doubted her. Unless they were me, that is.

Standing in the same place for long hours with nothing to do has very little to recommend it, except that it does give you plenty of time to think.

How had she done it?

I didn't doubt for a moment that the gem Julia smashed so dramatically in the Prince's audience chamber had been a duplicate which she somehow managed to switch for the genuine fire stone.

A number of factors had worked in her favour: clearly she had done her research, or been well briefed, and knew a great deal about fire stones – far more than anybody else around here at any rate. I had no idea how much of what she'd spouted regarding the stones' properties and history might be true and how much fanciful elaboration, but nor did anyone else, and that was the key. All she really needed to do was speak with sufficient authority that it *sounded* convincing, and that much she had achieved beyond reproach.

The sole aspect of her story I didn't doubt was the part about all the gems having been set in identical rings. How else could she have had a duplicate prepared in advance, ready to swap when the opportunity arose?

As for how the swap had been achieved, at first I suspected Julia may have infiltrated House Storm herself, using our little raid as a decoy. The captain, Turncoat and me, we were the stalking horses, there to draw attention while she slipped in unnoticed and swapped the rings ahead of us, so that it was the fake that I brought with me out of Storm. In this theory's favour was the coincidence of the fire that had broken out while we were there, drawing many of the guards away. Perhaps she had set that to give us a fighting chance.

On the other hand, that scenario would have required several unlikely acts on Julia's part: escaping the men guarding the priestess, dashing across town to arrive at House Storm ahead of us, gaining access without being seen, getting in and out of the guarded room where the ring was kept without raising an alarm, exiting House Storm – setting a fire along the way – before another cross-town dash in order to slip back into High Balvue and return to wherever she was supposed to have been all this while, without her absence being noted by any party.

Now I'm not saying any of that was beyond her, but surely it was far simpler to remain in High Balvue the whole while, conspicuously visible, and to then make the switch following my return. That still left the cause of the fire unresolved: a happy coincidence? Maybe, if you gave credence to such things.

I had, after all, placed the ring in the palm of her hand. The more I considered that moment, replaying it in my mind as she curled her fingers to collect the ring from her palm and bring it to her eye for scrutiny, the greater my conviction that the ring she then pretended to study was not the same one I had presented to her. There was all that business of pushing back her hood and picking up the loupe: in retrospect they struck me as distractions, staged to draw the eye of those around her for the split second it took to make the switch. All the while she spun her yarn of the fire stones and made such a show of examining the fake, the real ring had been safely hidden within the sleeve of her robe. Or perhaps she made the switch later still, when she placed the loupe and then the ring so precisely on the small table…

Either way, her final dramatic act ensured the switch would not be discovered; she had smashed the false stone, destroying the evidence and making certain that none of the jewellers the Prince had used to authenticate the fire stone could examine it and confirm this was *not* the same stone he had originally shown them.

It was bold and it was brazen, though neither word did her performance justice; masterful: that just about covered it.

The Tapered Eel was surprisingly quiet, for all that the evening was young, and I spotted the veteran almost immediately. He was indulging in the sort of dark mead I hated – too cloying and far too sweet. Armed with a tankard of the considerably lighter local ale, which was a little on the hoppy side for my taste but still markedly better than the mead, I pulled up a stool beside him.

"Here's to the conquering hero," he said, raising his drink in salute.

"Sod off."

"You did well," he said, no longer mocking.

"Oh yes, I excelled myself, no question about that: breaking into the enemy stronghold and defying a small army, all in order to reclaim a trinket that proved to be fake and worthless." I had no intention of sharing my suspicions regarding the Prince's Scarlene Priestess. "Not to mention getting our captain killed along the way… A triumph in every regard."

"Don't go selling yourself short, no one else is. You weren't to know the ring was a wrong 'un, none of us were. You did all that was asked of you against the odds, and that hasn't gone unnoticed by the Prince, trust me, which can't do you any harm at all." He lowered his voice and glanced around furtively before adding, "Besides, the loss of the Prince's nephew won't exactly damage the House."

"He was an honest and conscientious man," I said, feeling strangely compelled to defend the captain now that he was dead, perhaps because of the part I'd played in rendering him so.

"Never did have much time for honest men myself. Always found 'em to be too… inflexible."

I grunted. "Know what you mean."

"Now practical men like you and me," he continued, "we know that sometimes you have to hold your finger up in the wind, judge which direction it's blowin' and bend accordingly, or risk being broken in two."

Our gazes locked, just for a moment, and understanding passed between us. At least, I think it did. *Someone* on the inside had to have helped House Storm steal the ring in the first place. The veteran wasn't present when that happened, of course, he had been away escorting the decoy coach – a perfect alibi if ever one were needed. However, he'd already shown that he had others willing to work for him… Wheels within wheels; coats that had turned once and were always liable to do so again.

"Very true," I agreed after a slight pause. "Of course, now that House Storm has been breached and embarrassed by unknown intruders, the wind will be set against them in no small measure."

"You're not wrong there. Word is already spreading across town, despite their best efforts to deny the whole incident. The loss of face is likely to set 'em back for many a long year to come."

We sipped out respective beers in quiet contemplation for a moment, before he said with exaggerated casualness, "There's a vacancy as Guard Captain now, as you know."

I nodded and, guessing what he was angling at, assured him, "Well, you'll have my support if the Prince chooses to promote you."

"Me?" He seemed genuinely startled at the prospect. "No, lad, I prefer standing at the commander's shoulder whispering sage advice in 'is ear as needed. That way, some other mucker's there to take the blame when things go tits up." I couldn't fault his logic on that score. "Besides, word is that you're in line for the job," he added.

"Me?" My turn to be startled. "But I'm the new recruit, only just been taken on…"

"True, but you're also the Hero of Storm, you've proved yourself, and I'll grant that you've more sense than most."

"That's not what you said when we first met. 'None too bright' were the exact words as I recall."

"Yes, well… That was then. Thing is, I'd have your back, and the priestess put in a good word for you before she left, too…"

Thanks, Julia. I shook my head; this ridiculous idea needed scotching before it took hold. "Sorry, the notion is very flattering but I'm not interested. I tried being captain of a personal guard once before."

Visions of Rosalind, my then-employer's wife, flashed across my mind: stolen smiles as I guarded her on a shopping trip to her favourite bazaar; her eyes squeezed shut, head thrown back, the tendons of her neck straining as she writhed beneath me during our first passionate rendezvous; fleeting glances over her husband's shoulder; our very last kiss, her lips pressed against mine as she died on my blade, a short while after she had murdered her husband and tried to frame me for the deed…

"What happened?" the veteran asked.

"It didn't end well."

There's no question that being part of one of the big House's retinue has its advantages: regular meals, a decent wage, a roof over your head at night, and the respect that working for a Merchant Prince affords. One aspect of the job I was finding harder to adjust to was the lack of any privacy. The sleeping accommodation consisted of barracks, which meant sharing a room with a bunch of strangers. I never had been big on camaraderie, not even back in the 'good old days' with Gerard's band, and it didn't help that the young lad Jorge was in there with me. He seemed to assume that the fact we had mucked out horses together when I first arrived made us bosom buddies, and my new notoriety only spurred him on, making him more determined than ever to introduce me to his sister.

Maybe I shouldn't have been so swift to dismiss the notion of taking command of the guard after all: at least the captain is assigned his own room.

As it was, I couldn't sneak off to my lodgings to examine an object in private. Nor would I risk doing so while on sentry duty in the courtyard, where it was impossible to know who might be observing me from any one of four directions at any given time. No, my best bet was to do so here, in a public tavern, once the veteran had returned to High Balvue and left me to finish my ale in peace.

I waited a few more minutes after he had left, taking the opportunity to look around discretely, making sure none of the other patrons were from the House. Once satisfied that all were unknown to me, I reached into the same pocket where the ruby bracelet and other jewellery from House Storm resided and drew out a small square of green cloth, neatly folded. This was the true reason Julia had sought me out before her departure; she had palmed it to me as I kissed her hand in farewell.

Carefully unwrapping the cloth, I found within a small broach wrought in silver – delicate work consisting of a simple dagger resting on an oak leaf. I knew that emblem: the badge of a small town called Arden. A place I had sworn never to return to. Twice.

I realised immediately what Julia intended by this gift. It was both an invitation and a challenge.

Find me, if you dare.

About the Author

Ian Whates is the author of ten published novels (two co-written), two novellas, and seventy-odd short stories that have appeared in a variety of venues, including *Nightmare Magazine, Galaxy's Edge, Daily Science Fiction*, the science journal *Nature* and numerous anthologies.

In 2019 Ian received the Karl Edward Wagner Award from the British Fantasy Society, while his work has been shortlisted for the Philip K. Dick Award and on three occasions for BSFA Awards. He is a director and former chair of the British Science Fiction Association and is the editor of more than 40 anthologies, as well as editing PS Publishing's digital magazine *ParSec*.

In 2006 Ian founded award-winning independent publisher NewCon Press by accident.

ALSO FROM NEWCON PRESS

The Wild Hunt – Garry Kilworth

When Gods meddle in the affairs of mortals, it never ends well... for the mortals, at any rate. Steeped in ancient law, history and imagination, Garry Kilworth serves up an epic Anglo-Saxon saga featuring warriors, witches, giants, dwarfs, light elves and more, as a young warrior wrongly accused of patricide sets out to clear his name and regain his birthright.

Comet Weather – Liz Williams

Practical Magic meets *The Witches of Eastwick*. A tale of four fey sisters set in contemporary London, rural Somerset, and beyond. The Fallow sisters: scattered like the four winds but now drawn back together, united in their desire to find their mother, Alys, who disappeared a year ago. They have help, of course, from the star spirits and the no-longer-living, but such advice tends to be cryptic and far from dependable...

Dark Angels Rising – Ian Whates

All that stands between humanity and disaster is a notorious band of brigands cum folk heroes who disbanded a decade ago. Reunited, Leesa, Jen, Drake and their fellow Angels must prevent a resurrected Elder – last of a long dead alien race – from reclaiming the scientific marvels of its people and establishing itself as God over all humankind.

Queen of Clouds – Neil Williamson

Wooden automata, sentient weather, talking cats, compellant inks and a host of vividly realised characters provide the backdrop to this rich dark fantasy. Stranger in the city Billy Braid becomes embroiled in Machiavellian politics and deadly intrigue, as the weather insists on misbehaving, putting the Weathermakers Guild in an untenable position...

How Grim Was My Valley – John Llewellyn Probert

After waking up on the Welsh side of the Severn Bridge with no memory of who he is, a man embarks on an odyssey through Wales, bearing witness to the stories both the people and the land itself feel moved to tell him, all the while getting closer to the truth about himself.

www.newconpress.co.uk

www.ingramcontent.com/pod-product-compliance
Lightning Source LLC
Chambersburg PA
CBHW030239180626
46810CB00008B/3198